Daniel's Decision

Book 4 in the Emerald Springs Legacy

NICOLE FLOCKTON, author of
Masquerade and *Seducing Phoebe*

CRIMSON ROMANCE

F+W Media, Inc.

Published by
Crimson Romance
an imprint of F+W Media, Inc.
10151 Carver Road, Suite 200
Blue Ash, OH 45242. U.S.A.
www.crimsonromance.com

ISBN 10: 1-4405-7103-1
ISBN 13: 978-1-4405-7103-9
eISBN 10: 1-4405-7104-X
eISBN 13: 978-1-4405-7104-6

This is a work of fiction. Names, characters, corporations, institutions, organizations, events, or locales in this novel are either the product of the author's imagination or, if real, used fictitiously. The resemblance of any character to actual persons (living or dead) is entirely coincidental.

Cover art © iStockphoto.com/kupicoo and iStockphoto.com/Mac99

To my partners in crime on this journey:
Monica, Holley, Robyn, and Elley—thank you

Acknowledgments

To be part of a continuity is a unique experience and one that I have loved so much, I would do it all over again. Monica, Elley, Holley, and Robyn—thanks for coming on this journey. It's been a blast and an absolute honor! The fun discussions we had, especially about who had the cutest hero, always made me laugh. Just quietly—Daniel rules!

I want to thank Dorothy Coe and Ramon Lawrence OAM, the directors of Echoes in Canning Vale, Western Australia, for taking the time to show Jason and I around the Echoes facilities and allowing us to attend one of their sound and vibration sessions. Thank you for sharing your stories of the remarkable successes through your treatments. The experience is one we will never forget.

The information detailed in this story related to the gong/vibration therapy is as relayed to me during my visit, any errors are my own.

To Jennifer Lawler and Julie Sturgeon and Crimson Romance: thank you for thinking my passing idea was a good one and for giving us this opportunity. Julie, thank you for your insight and advice for improving my story and characters.

Tara Gelsomino, thank you for being so open and willing to listen to our suggestions to promote the continuity—your support has been amazing.

My readers, you are the reason I keep doing this, even though sometimes I feel like throwing the laptop out the window. Thank you for enjoying my stories. I love hearing from you.

As always, thank you to Jason and my kids—I love you!

Chapter 1

Daniel Whitman swirled the glass tumbler, watching the amber liquid circle and cling to the outer edges of the glass, the ice clinking against the sides in musical accompaniment. It did little to drown out the noise coming from the party going on behind him.

He should have been celebrating with the rest of his family. He was happy his little brother had found contentment and happiness in his life. Jen, his brother's fiancée, had made remarkable changes in Chad's wayward, fun-loving personality. Seems everyone around him was finding love—including his father. He took another gulp and welcomed the burn trickling down his throat.

What he felt like doing was buying a bottle of the twenty-year-old malt whiskey he was drinking and having his own private little party. Instead, he lifted his near-empty glass in a signal to the barman that he wanted a top-up.

"Everything all right, son?" his father asked as he slipped onto the empty barstool next to him.

Daniel raised his glass in a mock salute. "Absolutely, just having a quiet drink."

"You might want to go easy on that," Richard Whitman said as he inclined his head at the glass in Daniel's hand.

He let out a harsh laugh and downed the rest of the contents. "It's my first drink, Dad."

He felt rather than heard the heavy sigh his father let out. "Look, you're not still upset about the meeting this afternoon, are you? You know Adam and I thought long and hard about your expansion plans for the resort. We agree they have merit and will be a good idea in the future, but with the new microbrewery, we can't justify another large capital outlay."

Daniel loved his older brother, Adam. He had missed him while Adam was away carving out his own career in Los Angeles. But during that time, Daniel thought he and his father had grown close while they discussed ideas like streamlining some of the business practices and accounting procedures at Emerald Tea Farm, which had increased profits and productivity. Now with Adam back, it was like Dad had disregarded all those conversations and listened only to his firstborn. He knew it bothered Chad, too, but Chad had eventually talked the family into expanding the diner into a modern microbrewery. Maybe he could use this opportunity to plant the seed in Dad's mind that proceeding now with the plans for Emerald Paradise Resort was the way to go.

"You do realize, Dad, we are missing out on a niche market? When we had Michael Williams, the actor, staying at the resort, he loved the privacy. It was the first time in years he and his wife had been able to vacation where no paparazzi bothered them. Where they didn't have to worry about embarrassing pictures appearing in the press." As Daniel warmed to his topic, his earlier melancholy mood drifted away on the breeze. "If we add a few high-class facilities to the ones we already have and increase the services we offer in the spa, get something that makes our resort stand out from the rest of the resorts in the United States, I believe we'd be running at nearly full capacity year-round. Not to mention if we made a few other changes to our processes—heck, we could be totally eco and environmentally friendly. Those types of features appeal to the rich and famous."

"Son, these changes you're proposing don't sound cheap. How can you guarantee that if we lay out all this money, we will run at capacity? It's a big risk, and at present it's one I'm not prepared to take, especially with the new microbrewery expansion." Dad paused and picked up the drink the bartender had placed in front of him. "Besides, how do you propose we attract these *high-class* guests to the resort? If we publicize our products and services, we effectively neutralize our anonymity, which according to you, is the main drawing card for these guests."

"Word of mouth, Dad. I told Michael we were looking at making changes, and he said to let him know when we did. He'd come back and let all his friends know."

"I wish you'd waited a little longer before saying anything, Dan. I know you have control of the resort, but the final decision is still mine. I just think we need to take a little time and sort through all it will take to achieve this."

Daniel bit back the groan of frustration that threatened to burst out of him. Why couldn't his father see what a great business decision this was? He'd drawn up a business plan, worked out the costs of the few changes necessary to make the resort one hundred percent eco-friendly. And with Adam's knowledge, it would be so easy. The main backbone of his father's business had been organic—sheesh, Chad's microbrewery was going to be organic. The resort had been one of the first in Washington State to use the latest green technology. They treated him like he didn't know how to do anything. He was the one who had an MBA in business, for heaven's sake.

"Dad, we already have a good reputation as a resort that uses green energy, but we're getting a little tired. We need to freshen things up, offer new and innovative spa techniques. I can't say it enough; I want to draw a different crowd to the resort." Then Daniel plunged ahead with an idea he hadn't presented that afternoon to his father and brothers. "In addition to trying to find something new and innovative for the resort, I'm also looking at introducing holistic massages and therapies to help with the treatment of cancer. Mom would've loved this. She'd have been helping me do the research."

Damn straight she'd help. No doubt she'd have dug up information he'd never even consider looking for. Even after five years, he still missed her like crazy. He must have been the only kid in his school whose mom had been his best friend. Sheila Whitman had always had time for him—no matter how busy she was she'd sit with him. Listen to him. Encourage him. She always believed in him, always thought his ideas were fantastic. She had been his biggest champion.

God, he wished she was here right now. She'd be able to convince his father that Daniel's plans were exactly what the resort needed.

"Yes, I'm sure she would've loved that. She always believed that eating the organic fruit from our farm slowed her illness." His father's words were quiet and filled with admiration for the woman who'd tried with all her might to fight the insidious disease that had taken hold of her and had never let go.

Daniel nodded and took another sip of the whiskey, not needing the numbing sensation he had craved a half an hour ago. "There have been great leaps in using holistic treatments to help cancer patients recover from chemotherapy and radiation sessions. Doctors are adding everything from massages to herbal teas to acupuncture to diet changes, including eating totally organic produce, to cancer treatment plans. We have a chance to reach that market, too. We already know how eating organic can help cancer patients. We've got all of that at our fingertips with the orchards. But imagine if we introduced a technique or concept so unique no other resort in North America has ever seen the likes of it. It would really set us apart from everyone else. The possibilities are endless, Dad. Surely you can see that."

"Dan, I can't argue with anything you're saying. Of all my sons, you've been the one with the business acumen. You have ensured that Emerald Paradise Resort has always been profitable, and I couldn't be prouder of you. However, we just can't do it at the moment. Maybe in a year's time."

"In a year's time it will be too late. Other resorts are already starting to make these changes. I've been trying to speak to the marketing manager at a resort in far north Queensland in Australia but haven't had any luck yet. According to their website, they're an eco-friendly resort and their spa is the best in the country. I thought about taking a trip down there to check it out."

"That's a long way to go. I'm sure there are other resorts in the United States that will give you everything you need."

"You've seen the research I presented to you earlier, we're on par with the resorts here in the States. But I don't want to be the same as the others. I want Emerald Paradise to be the best, and this Australian resort is an award-winning, world-class operation; we could learn a lot from them."

"Richard, darling, are you ready to go?" A light feminine voice interrupted their conversation.

Daniel gripped his glass a little tighter. He still found it hard to believe his father and their housekeeper, Patty, were now an item. His father loving another woman. A woman who wasn't his mother. The idea seemed so foreign to him.

He kept his eyes focused on his hands and not on what he was sure would be Patty touching his father's arm.

"Give me a couple more minutes, sweetheart, then I'll be ready to go."

"Okay, I'll go wait with Zoe. Bye Daniel."

Daniel tried not to flinch when he heard the sound of lips meeting in a quick kiss. He needed to get out of there. There was no point continuing with the conversation. It was a dead end. He placed his glass back on the bar, pulled a couple of bills out of his wallet, and threw them down.

"It's okay, Dad, I'm leaving now anyway." He couldn't deny the happiness shining on his father's face. It didn't mean he had to like it, though. "I'll see you both later."

He turned and walked away, not bothering to say goodbye to his brothers. He was sure they'd give him hell over it later, but at the moment he didn't care. He just needed to get away.

The cool night air hit him and he welcomed its freshness. He'd walked to the restaurant, as he knew it wouldn't be a good idea for him to drive home after a few drinks. He used the time to clear his head and work out what his next move would be.

There were so many changes going on around him. Both of his brothers were now engaged. His father was in love with his housekeeper. Even Colleen, the daughter of his father's former business partner, had fallen in love and was expecting a baby. She'd been the last person he, and everyone else in town, had expected to succumb to Cupid's clutches. It appeared there was something in the water in Emerald Springs, and he planned to stay as far away from it as possible. The very idea of falling in love and getting married was anathema to him.

Footsteps sounded behind him, but he didn't bother turning to see who was there. Lots of people walked the streets at night. Emerald Springs was a safe place; he had no need to worry about anything bad happening. But he did up his pace a fraction, surprised when the person behind him also sped up.

His immediate response was to turn and check out who was following him. He would've if he wasn't a short distance away from his house. An uneasy feeling settled over him. He jogged at night and had never experienced any problems. Why was he worried about the walk home? To see what would happen, he again increased his pace. The person behind him did the same.

This was definitely unusual.

He reached the front door of his house as his phone rang. Over the tone, he heard a muffled curse. He turned quickly to see someone darting across the street.

What the hell?

Shaking his head in disbelief, he pulled his cell out of his pocket along with his keys, and glanced at the caller ID as he unlocked the door.

Adam.

The last thing he wanted was to talk to his older brother. What he really wanted to do was catch up with the suspicious person, demand to know what the hell he wanted and why he felt the need to follow him. But Daniel knew if he didn't answer, both his brothers would be camped on his doorstep first thing in the morning.

"Hey Adam, what's up?"

"You tell me, Daniel. You left Chad and Jen's engagement celebration without saying goodbye. That's not like you; so what gives?"

Daniel sighed; it was never good when Adam called him *Daniel*. He closed his door and walked down the hallway, his footsteps echoing around him. His house seemed quiet and lonely.

"Nothing, man, I'm just tired."

Even to his own ears he didn't sound convincing, and there was no way Adam was going to let him get away with it.

"I saw you talking to Dad. Tell me you're not still annoyed about the resort plans. It's just not—"

"I know, I know, it's just not good timing," he interrupted his brother. "I heard it from Dad again tonight. The fact you guys can't see how this will improve the overall profit margin of the organization baffles me. You've both made your decision, but it doesn't mean I have to agree with it or like it or even follow it."

"What have you got planned, little brother?" Suspicion laced Adam's every word.

"Nothing." Daniel ran his fingers through his hair. He wanted off the phone. "Nothing at all. Look I need to go. I'll speak to you later. Bye."

Adam's goodbye faded as Daniel pulled the phone away from his ear. He tossed it and his keys onto the coffee table, right on top of the plans he'd shown to his family this afternoon. He sat down on the couch and picked them up. Every time he looked at them, he got excited. The possibilities were endless.

His phone buzzed for a second time, and he knew who it would be without having to check caller ID. He picked it up and connected the call.

"Hey, Chad, I'm fine."

His younger brother's chuckle drifted down the line. "I should be mad at you for slinking out on me. I had so much more fun planned for you. One of Jen's friends was eyeing you earlier. Seems she likes the brooding, silent *business-suit* type. Guess there's no accounting for taste."

"Bro, I *don't* need you to do any matchmaking, thanks. I can find my own dates; I've never had to rely on you or Adam to set me up."

"What about Becky and her sister, Trina?"

Daniel burst out laughing. He could always count on Chad to lighten his mood. "Man, that was the date from hell, and besides, you tricked me into going with you."

"Who knew Trina was an octopus in disguise?"

Daniel recalled how Trina's hands seemed to have a life of their own—all over his body. "Well I don't plan on falling into the trap you and Adam did. I've got my life planned out and getting married isn't even listed on the pages at present."

"Famous last words, bro, famous last words. It's contagious you know. Even the old man got hit."

Just like that, Daniel's good mood evaporated. He didn't need any reminders about his father and Patty. "Yeah, well, not happening here. I've got too much to do before I'd even consider entering into a serious relationship with someone."

Daniel reached out and woke up the laptop sitting on his coffee table. A picture of a stunning wooden structure surrounded by lush green trees filled his screen. An idea quickly flared to life. He wanted to get away, and what better place to do that than at the resort he wanted Emerald Paradise Resort to emulate? Since Kulang Resort was on the other side of the world, it was the perfect getaway from all the sickening happiness surrounding him lately. Without a solid plan in place, without doing all the research necessary, Daniel acted solely on his need to disappear for a while and made a decision. "Listen, Chad, I'm going to take a trip. I'll probably be gone for a couple of weeks. When I get there I'll call you."

"Whoa, man, what?"

If anyone could understand his frustrations, it would be Chad. Chad had fought tooth and nail for his business expansion plans. The fact that the microbrewery had put Daniel's resort on the back burner should have annoyed him, but he was proud of his little brother, and he couldn't hold it against him.

"I need to get away, bro. I need some space to deal with everything that's happening around here. I just can't deal with seeing—"

"Okay, I get it," Chad interrupted. "Look, just let me know when you get to wherever you're going, and I'll break the news to Dad and Adam that you've done a runner."

"I'm not doing a runner; I'm going on a scouting trip."

"I don't want to know. The less information I have, the less trouble I'll get into. I hope," Chad said on a laugh. "I got your back, Dan."

"Thanks, Chad, I owe you."

"Yeah you do, big time, bro. Take care."

As Chad disconnected the call, Daniel opened Google and typed in Travelocity. Half an hour later, he had his flights and accommodation booked. In two days, he'd be in Australia inspecting Kulang Resort. He would make the changes to his resort even if he had to take out a second mortgage on his house to complete them. He believed in his vision, and he would do whatever it took to bring it to life.

• • •

Rochelle Harris rearranged the flowers on the reception desk, removing some blooms that were wilting. The perfume from the lilies was subtle but refreshing. She straightened a magazine and gave a slight nod, satisfied that the area looked neat but welcoming.

She loved her job. There was nothing more fulfilling than seeing people enter the resort tired and in desperate need of relaxation and then checking out with an abundance of energy and eager to book their next visit. Knowing she played a little part in making their stay enjoyable and that her innovative marketing techniques drew guests to the resort made all her hard work and the sacrifices she'd made along the way to get into the management position she now held, all worthwhile.

It wasn't hard to relax, not when surrounded by the healthy rainforest and treatments meant to restore a weary soul. Even she made sure to book a weekly hot stone massage to ensure her energy levels were constantly on an even keel.

As Rochelle gave the reception area another once over, she noticed a man walking into the resort. He strode confidently through the doors; she pegged him for a successful businessman. He probably had a glossy, perfectly made-up woman following behind.

Except he didn't. He didn't waver in his strides, as if he was waiting for someone to catch up with him.

She made her way a bit closer to the reception desk. It wasn't unusual but it definitely wasn't common for a single man to come to the resort. She moved behind the counter, smiling at one of the staff as she did so.

"Good morning, sir, and welcome to Kulang Resort."

Rochelle smiled as she heard the front desk clerk greet the mystery guest. She had no idea why she was so interested in him, but he'd piqued her curiosity. She risked a glance at him then looked quickly away. Up close, he was even more magnetic. She tried to ignore the increase in her heart rate. She wasn't normally one to like a five o'clock shadow on a man, but on this guest it was extremely sexy.

She pushed the thought away. It was her personal policy not to get involved with any guest. The owners of Kulang had no hard and fast rule about guests and staff. But for her, getting involved with a guest could be detrimental to her career. She'd made that mistake once, and she wasn't going to do it again.

"Good morning, my name's Daniel Whitman and I have a reservation."

Daniel Whitman.

Why did that name ring a bell? She racked her brain, trying to see if there was something that would trigger her memory. He was American; she got that from his accent.

Was he a returning guest? No, she didn't think he was. But then again, it wasn't like she knew all the guests who had ever stayed at the resort.

Daniel Whitman.

She knew that name, she was sure of it, and it was bugging her that she couldn't remember how she knew him.

"I see you haven't booked in for any of the treatments the resort offers, Mr. Whitman. Is there something in particular you'd like to experience?"

"I haven't made up my mind, but when I do, I'll let you know. Your resort has so much to offer; it's almost too hard to choose."

There was nothing in what he said that should have unlocked her memory, but she suddenly knew who Daniel Whitman was. He was the person who had been emailing her to get information about the resort. She'd not responded because she wasn't sure if his claim as a resort owner was legitimate. She had been too caught up with the new marketing and expansion plans she'd been working on to take time to do proper research on the resort he said he was from, and until she'd looked more carefully into his background, she wasn't going to respond to his queries.

Now was the perfect opportunity to find out why he was here and what he wanted from her. If he wanted anything. She took a step forward and held out her hand toward him.

"Good morning, Mr. Whitman, I'm Rochelle Harris, marketing manager at Kulang Resort. You've been emailing me, right?"

Rochelle wasn't prepared for the sensations that shot through her the moment Daniel grasped her hand. It took everything in her to shake his hand professionally and not pull away and tuck her own hand behind her back.

"Ms. Harris, finally we connect." His voice had lowered fractionally and the hint of a smile he sent her way did nothing to quell the feelings that were starting to override her good sense.

He sounded so calm, as if their hands touching didn't affect him in any way. It probably didn't; it was probably nothing new to him. She was sensitive to the reasons why he had been emailing her, not because of her earlier admiration of him when he'd entered the resort.

Rochelle extracted her hand from his hold. "I wouldn't say connect, Mr. Whitman, but welcome to the resort. I hope you enjoy your stay with us."

He looked her up and down, and she worked hard to control the slow rise of heat she could feel building inside of her.

"Everything I've seen so far leads me to believe I'm going to enjoy my time here very much."

"Excellent. If you need anything, please don't hesitate to contact any of our staff. We'll be more than happy to help you decide on any of the services we offer. We do have a range of treatments especially designed for our male guests. Enjoy your stay, Mr. Whitman."

Rochelle moved away from the desk and from the man who had screwed up her equilibrium.

She reached the safety of her office and closed the door. Leaning against the solid wood, she took a few deep breaths. Never before had a guest rattled her like Daniel Whitman had. But he wasn't a guest in the true sense of the word. She'd been caught out once before by thinking someone was a guest when in fact they'd been there to use her and her knowledge. She wasn't getting caught out this time though. She knew from the emails Daniel Whitman was from a rival resort. He wasn't there to relax. He was visiting to scope out Kulang's facilities. She would make sure she kept out of his way for the duration of his stay. If he had any questions, she would refer them to her assistant, Melanie. It probably wasn't the most professional thing to do, but it was the only way she knew she could handle the situation.

For the sake of her career, and to keep her focus on her goal to learn everything she could about running a resort so she could be appointed General Manager and run it one day, she had to be sensible. She could not get distracted by an attraction to someone who could ruin it all. Avoiding Daniel Whitman was a top priority now.

Chapter 2

Daniel had noticed Rochelle Harris the moment she appeared in his peripheral vision as he was checking in. He'd noticed how attractive she was. Her blonde hair was caught up in a side ponytail exposing her long neck, something he found extremely sexy. Her dress hugged her body accentuating her curves. She was no sex kitten though. Her eyes shone with intelligence and insight. He had no doubt a conversation with her would be fascinating. For the first time in months his body had stirred to life. He hadn't been prepared for the flare of attraction that sparked between them when he took her hand in his. He was sure she'd felt it, too, because of the way she'd backed away from him and ended their conversation. He knew a brush off when he saw one. He wasn't going to let her get away with it though. From the brief research he'd done, he knew Rochelle was the one who had made the changes to Kulang Resort's website and marketing brochures, highlighting the eco-side of the resort. The exclusivity of the location along with the combination of spa packages to tempt the tired guest were small but effective enticements, taking Kulang from an ordinary resort to an extraordinary one. She was the key, and he would do whatever it took to get her advice on the improvements he needed to make at Emerald Paradise Resort.

First he would arrange a meeting with her, introduce himself properly, and talk a little about why he was visiting Kulang. Perhaps he could tempt her into having dinner with him and get to know Rochelle over food and wine, while at the same time try to entice information out of her. With a concise plan of action in his mind, he strode over to the phone and dialed the front desk.

"Reception, how can I help you?"

"I'd like to be put through to Ms. Harris, please."

"I'm sorry, sir, Ms. Harris has placed a hold on all her calls. I can put you through to her assistant, and you can leave a message if you wish."

"Yes, that would be helpful, thanks."

Daniel drummed his fingers on the side table as he waited for his call to be connected. He should be feeling tired. Instead, he felt energized, even though he'd been unable to get a seat in business class after booking on such short notice, so sleep had eluded him on the almost twenty-hour flight.

"This is Melanie, how can I help you?" He had no reaction to the soft, feminine voice. Yet the smoky tone and single touch from Rochelle Harris earlier had made his body come alive. "Yes, I'd like to make an appointment to see Ms. Harris, today if possible."

"That shouldn't be a problem, sir. She has some time available in half an hour. Will that work for you?"

Half an hour would be perfect; it would give him enough time to shower and change. "Yes, that's fine, thank you."

He hung up before she could ask his name. He instinctively knew that if Rochelle saw he made the appointment, she wouldn't be in her office when he arrived.

Sure it was sneaky, but nothing about this trip was normal. Normally he didn't run away from his problems. But taking a spur-of-the-moment research trip to the other side of the world behind his father's back, could be constituted as running away by some people.

Right on time he stood outside Rochelle's office door. He'd sweet-talked Melanie into letting him go in unannounced, implying that Rochelle had invited this meeting at check-in and was now expecting him.

He raised his hand and gave one brisk knock before twisting the handle and opening the door. The look of shock on Rochelle's face was priceless. Yes, he was going to enjoy this trip immensely.

• • •

Rochelle almost dropped the phone when Daniel burst through her door. She quickly finished her conversation and hung up. What was he doing here? Did he think he could just come in unannounced? Well he had another think coming. No way was she going to be bullied into giving him information.

"Mr. Whitman, this is a surprise. I have someone coming in a few min … " her voice trailed off as she realized just who her next appointment was. The smile that broke out over his face confirmed her suspicions. "You're my next appointment, aren't you?"

"Yes."

Rochelle clasped her hands together and inclined her head. "Why don't you take a seat? What is it you wish to discuss with me, Mr. Whitman, that you had to go to such secret measures?"

"Would you have seen me if I had told your assistant my name?"

She had to concede his point, but she wasn't going to admit it to him. "Well you'll never know now, will you?"

He laughed and the sound drifted slowly down her spine like a feather wafting on a breeze. "I guess I won't."

She turned her attention to her computer and scrolled through her inbox until she came across his last email. She scanned the contents before she addressed him again.

"So, Mr. Whitman, from your emails it appears you're looking at expanding the services your resort offers, is that right?"

She was pleased with how professional she sounded. He didn't need to know that her heart was pounding double time.

"It's Daniel, and yes."

"Pardon?"

"Please call me Daniel. Mr. Whitman is my father. And yes, I want to expand the services Emerald Paradise offers so we can attract a higher class clientele."

"Well it will take a little more than just expanding your treatments to lure the clientele you're after. You will have to ensure your resort is the best in every way from the staff to the linens you use, to the food you serve in your resort restaurant, if you have one—; it all has to be top quality, etc., etc."

"I already have those things in place. Kulang is a world-renowned eco-friendly resort, and I want mine to be that as well. All the produce we use is organic, and we are making the necessary changes to convert to green energy."

"When it comes to the eco side of things, I'm not sure I'm qualified to help you with that. I'm in charge of Kulang's marketing and sourcing the latest in treatments. You'll have to speak to the general manager about those other aspects."

"That's fine. The eco side of things isn't the major reason for my trip, but I will make time to talk to him." As he leaned forward, Rochelle moved her chair back a fraction. Even though her desk separated them, she still felt he was intruding on her personal space. "What I'd really like to do is have dinner with you."

The invitation was so out of the blue; she opened and closed her mouth like a fish out of water. Her instinctive response was to say yes. It would be nice to have a conversation with someone for a change, instead of watching mindless television shows while she ate her dinner. Her sensible side realized it wouldn't be wise to have dinner with him. He could seriously derail her equilibrium with his sexy smile and seductive eyes. Tempting her when she couldn't let herself be tempted. He was a competitor and she needed to keep that fact at the fore front of her mind. She couldn't afford another slip-up with a rival resort employee, no matter how delicious he looked. "I don't think that's a good idea."

"Why not?"

She sighed. It was clear he wasn't going to take no for an answer. She had to be more convincing.

"Daniel, you are a guest at the resort. It's not a written rule—more implied you could say—" She was bending the truth here, but he didn't have to know it was her own preference rather than the management's—"but it's inappropriate for staff to socialize with the guests after hours."

"I'm not your normal guest; I'm here on business. As the owner of a resort, I'm reviewing the practices of a colleague. Don't tell me you don't have a specific employee who visits your competitors to see what they're offering."

She couldn't argue with that logic. She did have someone who travelled around Australia doing exactly that. Still, the last time she'd had dinner with a guest, it had almost killed her career. She learned too late he was a spy, just like Daniel.

"Well, yes, we do, but our employee doesn't seek out the competition's marketing managers and ask them out to dinner. They're more inclined to check out the facilities themselves and then move on."

"I've never been one to follow the rules."

"Really? I never would've guessed," she replied sweetly. If she were being honest with herself, she'd have to admit she was enjoying this exchange with Daniel. It had been a long time since she'd felt the urge to flirt with someone of the opposite sex.

That thought pulled her up short. She shouldn't be feeling this way around him. There was no way this could go anywhere, and she had no business thinking it possibly could. She wasn't going to let anyone steer her off the course she had mapped out for her life: a house, an investment portfolio, financial security.

Rochelle wasn't sure what to do when Daniel stood and moved around to her side of the desk, resting his hip on it. He crossed his arms and he looked decidedly sexy and dangerous. Everything she didn't need right at that moment.

"So the question is, Rochelle," he leaned down closer into her personal space, "are you a rule follower?"

There was nothing but pure challenge in his voice and question. It was one challenge she should back away from quickly. However, this pull was too strong and she wanted to give into the temptation he presented.

"Depends on the rules."

This time it was he who quirked his eyebrow. "Really? I am intrigued. So which rules do you break?"

The flirty part of her that had lain dormant for so long, until this meeting with Daniel, reared its head. She crooked her finger and beckoned him closer. When he was within inches of her lips, she whispered, "Sometimes I drive over the speed limit."

He burst out laughing, and she had to admit she quite liked the sound. His eyes were twinkling with merriment. He was so close. The temptation to reach out and trace his lips with her finger was strong. The desire to place her lips on his was even stronger. She fought against it. Dinner would be such a bad idea. Such a bad, bad idea.

"Your secret is safe with me." He moved away and Rochelle couldn't help feeling a little colder at the loss of his warmth. As he took his seat, she saw fatigue had replaced the merriment that shone so brightly in his eyes only moments ago. It hit her then that he had probably been travelling for a long time and was, more than likely, suffering from jet lag. "Does that mean you'll come to dinner with me?"

She sighed. He clearly wouldn't stop until he got what he wanted. Maybe it would be best to have one dinner with him and then he would leave her alone.

"Fine, yes, I will have dinner with you."

"I have a feeling there is a 'but' in there."

She laughed lightly. "Yes, there is. I will have dinner with you tonight, *but* it's a business meeting, and it will be a one-night-only affair."

"Oh, honey, believe me, it won't be a one night only affair." He stood and headed toward her door, pausing before he turned the handle. "You'll find out one night won't be enough for you, either."

He walked out before she had time for a quick comeback. But somehow she knew his words were prophetic. One night with Daniel wouldn't be enough, and that was going to be very, very dangerous for her soul.

•••

There was a lightness in Daniel's step as he headed back to his room. The banter with Rochelle had fired his blood. He'd never gone toe-to-toe with a woman in the way he had with Rochelle. She sassed him back; most other women he dated usually laughed and batted their eyelids at him. He found the intellectual side of Rochelle very, very tantalizing. The practical part of his brain was telling him that now was the worst possible time for him to consider any sort of affair with a woman. He needed his focus on the plans he wanted to implement for his business. He'd seen what happened with Chad and Jen as their relationship had blossomed among the blueprints for the microbrewery at Emerald Eats. It had almost ended in a major disaster because Chad had lost his focus. The fact that Chad was blissfully happy with Jen now was beside the point. He wasn't Chad though, and he could deal with a little harmless flirtation like the one he and Rochelle had embarked on. He certainly wasn't going to let it develop into anything like what Chad and Jen or Adam and Zoe now had. He wasn't so stupid as to fall in love.

Famous last words, bro, famous last words. Careful, it's contagious, you know.

Chad's words from their last phone conversation played loudly in his mind. No, Daniel wasn't going to get blinded by the attraction he'd felt toward Rochelle. It had been a while since he'd been with a woman; that was the only reason he was reacting to her.

Speaking of Chad, he'd promised to call his brother when he arrived. Checking his watch, he made a quick calculation and worked out that it wasn't too late in the evening in Emerald Springs to call him. Daniel picked up his cell phone and scrolled through his contacts until he found Chad's name, then tapped his screen to connect the call.

It seemed to take forever before Chad picked up his call; Daniel fully expected it to go to voicemail, and then he'd have to leave a message.

"Hey, Dan."

"Hey, bro, wanted to let you know I made it to Australia."

"Australia? What the hell? Actually, I don't want to know."

There was something about Chad's response that seemed out of character for his brother.

"Is everything okay, Chad? Did Dad and Adam give you a hard time about my leaving?"

It was then Daniel heard some giggling in the background and realized he had more than likely interrupted Chad and Jen.

"I've caught you at a bad time, haven't I? Doesn't matter, I wanted to let you know that I got here in one piece. I'll call you later."

He disconnected before Chad had a chance to respond. His lighter mood dissipated like the fog rolling over the green tea fields of the family farm. He tossed the phone down, walked over to the bed, and flopped down.

Fatigue gripped him hard. If he was going to be alert at dinner, he needed either sleep or another shower to wake him up. He knew if he grabbed some winks now, he'd probably not sleep later on that night. So a shower it was.

As he undressed, he admired his room décor. The colors were soft and muted, eliciting an atmosphere of tranquility. The theme had been carried into the bathroom as well. Even the complimentary shampoo and conditioner were organic. So, the room's amenities were pretty much the same as what he offered at his resort. At least he had that right, although he could freshen the paint in the rooms, update the furnishings, and maybe get some new linens for the resort. Minor changes that wouldn't disrupt the bookings they had. But he needed something unique to add to Emerald Paradise. Something that would be a great drawing card for guests, and if it could somehow be connected to helping cancer patients, that would be a dream come true. Hopefully something would show up during his visit and he could take it back and prove to everyone that his business acumen was as good as Dad's.

As he started to get into the shower, he heard a knock on his door. He contemplated ignoring it. The warm water was calling him, but another knock, this time a little more insistent, made up his mind.

Cursing, he turned off the water, grabbed a towel, and wrapped it around his waist. He made his way to the door and pulled it open with more force than was necessary. His quick reflexes caught Rochelle as she almost fell into the room from where she was standing with one hand on the doorframe while the other was replacing her shoe.

As he righted her he couldn't help but notice the softness of her skin under his hand. He wondered if she was soft all over. Her breasts brushed up against his chest.

"Umm, sorry." The words rushed out of Rochelle as she pulled away from his hold.

He wanted to draw her back into his arms and kiss her, lead her to the bed, and lose himself in her lush body. His body flared to life at the thought, and his towel wasn't a decent enough barrier against his cock standing to attention. Instead, he crossed his arms across his chest in a classic defensive pose, hoping to keep her gaze above his waist. "That's fine, what can I do for you?" Her eyes widened at his cool tone.

"Well, you left before I could ask what time you wanted to meet for dinner. I'm assuming you want to stay at the resort?"

"Yes dinner here at the resort would be my first choice, unless you know of a better place.

"No, here's fine; it makes sense. Why don't you come by my—," her hesitation had him standing a little straighter. "—office at say, 6:30 p.m.? I'll make a reservation at the resort restaurant for about 6:45 p.m. Will that work?"

There was something she wasn't telling him and Daniel couldn't quite put his finger on it. If he weren't suffering from jet lag, he probably would pick up what it was straight away.

"Sure, that will work."

"Great, well … " she waved her hand toward his bare chest and he had to suppress the chuckle threatening to erupt. "I'll let you get back to what you were doing."

She was out of his room, closing the door behind her before he had a chance to react. He stood for a few moments looking at the back of his door. Rochelle Harris was an intriguing mix of professional woman and sexy ingénue. Somehow by the time he left to head back to Emerald Springs he would know her body intimately, even though getting involved was a bad idea. For once in his life he was going with flow, no matter what the outcome.

• • •

Rochelle took a couple of steps down the hallway before leaning against the wall, closing her eyes and jamming a fist into her mouth to stave off the moan of frustration she could feel building inside her.

Daniel's *sleepy* eyes and low-slung towel danced behind her closed eyelids. It was an image she knew was going to stay with her for a long while. Strong, muscular chest, with a definite six-pack, glowing in the soft light of his hotel room. A smattering of dark-colored hair, just enough to be attractive and not offensive.

It was such a bad idea to have dinner with him, but she found that her feet wouldn't move back to his room so she could tell him she'd changed her mind. She could, of course, leave a message for him on his room phone, but that seemed a cowardly way out. She headed for her employee apartment in the opposite direction instead.

At least having him collect her from her office would keep things professional. It would be the worst thing possible for him to know she was living on site, in close proximity to him.

She was going to change that though. Soon she'd be able to put a deposit down on a nice little bungalow she could call home. A place of her own where she could create the tranquil living area she'd always wanted. A place of her own that her mother couldn't touch. A place of her own that could never be taken away from her.

As she let herself into her small apartment, she headed straight for her bedroom. It would be sensible to stay in the plain scoop neck dress she was wearing, but part of her wanted to look her best for her dinner date with Daniel.

It's not a date, a little voice inside of her mind yelled. *Remember your focus. Don't let a man sway you from your end goal. Love only leads to betrayal and hurt.*

She shushed the voice, even though what it was telling her was what she needed to remember. Still, she had a bit of feminine pride, and she did want to look good. It was what she would do for any work dinner she had to attend, which is what she'd arranged with Daniel—a business dinner to discuss the resort's features. It could never be a date.

But her heart was taking no notice of what her mind was saying.

Chapter 3

Daniel was late.

Rochelle never thought he would stand her up. Then again, he'd been cold toward her when he was in his room. She plucked at the short hemline of her dress and felt like a fool. The black dress screamed sexy, not business attire.

What was she thinking?

Even though the staff was discreet, word was sure to get around that she was fraternizing with a guest. It could be career suicide.

She stopped pacing around her office and picked up her purse. If Daniel Whitman was going to stand her up, she wasn't going to be here to take it. She was going back to her apartment to heat up a packet of two-minute noodles and watch crappy reality television until she was brain dead.

She pulled open her door and gave a small yelp when Daniel's loosely clenched fist connected with her forehead. "Ouch."

His laughter rumbled through the room and she glared up at him. "Really, you laugh? You could've knocked me out," she cried indignantly.

That only seemed to make him laugh more. Okay, so she'd been over-reacting. "Fine, you probably wouldn't have knocked me out but"—she rubbed the tender spot on her forehead as she laughed—"it did hurt ... a little."

"How about I make it feel better?"

Rochelle had no time to react as Daniel leaned forward and placed a soft kiss on the place she had been rubbing just seconds ago. Heat radiated through the tiny bump on her head, all the way down her spine. Her fingertips tingled and itched to reach up and bring his head down to her lips.

She took a step back. "Uh, thanks, but it doesn't hurt now."

He gave her a cheeky smile that melted her already wobbly legs. "See, I told you I could make you feel better."

His arrogance should have annoyed her. With any other male it usually did. She'd dealt with many men just like him in her position as marketing manager. It hadn't taken them long to realize that she wasn't the helpless little girl they all thought her to be.

"Yes, well … " her voice trailed off as she finally took notice of his appearance. He was wearing black trousers, a black shirt that fitted snugly but not so much that it looked like it was three sizes too small. "You're late," she blurted out, not knowing where the words came from. She sounded like a putout child after someone had taken her favorite toy and replaced it with a rubber band.

Daniel took a step into the room and closed the door. At least someone was thinking straight. Although it was unlikely anyone would see them as most of the people who worked near her office had long gone home.

"Yeah, sorry about that. I rested my eyes for a moment and woke up half an hour later."

Sympathy filled her as she took notice of the tired lines around his eyes and mouth. She should cancel the dinner appointment and make a time to meet him in her office tomorrow. It would be best for all involved.

"Look," she started. "If you're too tired, we can postpone and have our meeting tomorrow."

"You'd leave a hungry man to go to bed without any sustenance?"

Rochelle had a feeling Daniel wasn't talking about food. If she were being totally honest with herself, she didn't want to cancel. For the first time in a while, she was enjoying sparring with someone. The fact that he was drop dead gorgeous certainly helped the situation.

"Well, when you put it like that, far be it from me to ignore the pleas of a hungry man." She moved toward her desk and picked up her iPad. She figured if she took her work tools with her, she'd remember that it wasn't a social evening. No matter how gorgeous he was, she couldn't let that sway her, even though it was extremely tempting to throw caution to the wind and imagine they were, in fact, embarking on a first date.

Daniel inclined his head toward the device in her hand. "I don't think you'll be needing that."

She walked towards him and opened her door again. "Quite the opposite, actually, Mr. Whitman. This is a business meeting, isn't it?"

You keep telling yourself that. The cynical voice inside of her head sounded loud and annoying.

"Well if you insist, *Ms. Harris,*" he said emphasizing the formal use of her name. Somehow it sounded sexy and not business like at all.

"Great, after you then." She swept out her arm, signaling him to precede her out the door.

"This is going to be some business meeting," he muttered under his breath as he walked past.

Rochelle chose to ignore the little jibe. She had a feeling it was going to take everything she had to keep their dinner on a professional level.

The moment they walked through the restaurant doors, Rochelle knew she'd made a big mistake thinking they could conduct a meeting here. The lights were low, and the room practically screamed romance. In all the years she'd worked at the resort, she hadn't eaten a single dinner in the restaurant. If anything, she ate in her apartment or made the half-hour drive to the nearest town to get a meal there. She'd had no reason to entertain at the restaurant in the evening; all her meetings were conducted in the resort boardroom or her office.

"Well now, isn't this cozy?"

There was nothing even remotely sarcastic in his words, but she bristled at the tone nonetheless. "We pride ourselves on creating a nice, relaxing atmosphere for our guests."

"Do you often conduct business meetings . . . ," his eye roved over her outfit, and she braced herself for what was to come next. "Dressed like that?"

Oh why did she think it was a good idea to change her clothes?

Before she could answer, he continued, "By the way, do you always keep clothes like that in your office for last minute meetings?"

Rochelle stiffened at the insinuation in his voice. She was getting whiplash from the way he flipped from flirty to arrogant. Luckily, she was saved from making an inappropriate retort by the maître d's arrival. "Good evening, Ms. Harris. This is an unexpected pleasure."

"Hi, Greg, I have a booking here this evening with Mr. Whitman, who's visiting from a resort in the USA."

She was proud of the professional sound in her voice, assuring Greg that this was indeed a business meeting and nothing more.

Greg nodded and looked at the computer screen in front of him. "Yes, we have a table in the corner for you." He stepped away from the small dais he stood behind. "Please follow me."

"Excellent, thank you." She sounded cheerful, although she was anything but as she followed Greg toward the corner, which was the last place Rochelle wanted to be. Had they been seated in the middle of the room, everyone would have observed her using her iPad and realized there was nothing untoward about the dinner.

She bit her lip as Daniel's hand landed at the small of her back. She almost stumbled but managed to regain her stride and follow Greg to the table.

After Greg held out her chair and placed menus in front of them, he moved away and silence descended over the table.

Needing something to do, Rochelle picked up her menu and perused the entrees.

"So what do you recommend for me?"

She peered over the top of her menu and met Daniel's gaze. His eyes glittered in the ambient light from the candle glowing subtly in the middle of the table. Looked like Mr. Flirty was back. She could handle Mr. Flirty. If Mr. Arrogant showed his head again, she was liable to walk out and make an even bigger fool of herself.

"I don't normally eat here, but I can assure you everything on this menu is first class. We only employ the best staff here."

"You being one of them?" he asked.

She was glad for the muted light as she felt the slow rise of heat starting at the bottom of her neck. Would he think her full of herself if she said yes? Well, it didn't matter. She was proud of her achievements and had nothing to be ashamed of.

"Yes. I've been in my current position for almost two years, and in that time we've doubled our bookings. Not to mention we've added a lot of the new initiatives I've come up with. I am excellent at my job."

She wondered what was going through Daniel's mind as he sat back and observed her. He had come to Kulang wanting to know why the resort was the best in the world, and she was the best person to give him that information.

When a smile broke out over his face, she gripped the menu a little tighter. His smile should come with a warning. It was lethal.

"I have no problems with anyone promoting their achievements. To get to the top of a career, you have to have confidence. Congratulations." He dropped his head back to the menu. "So I ask again: what can you recommend? What are you going to order?"

Rochelle dropped her gaze back to the black folder she was holding, enjoying the warmth flowing through her at his compliment. She was especially excited about a new project she was hoping to present to the board. There was no way she was going to mention it to Daniel though. Never again would she share her visions with anyone not associated with her resort, especially this one. She wanted Kulang Resort to be the first resort in the world to offer the complementary alternative medicine facility she had found.

"I'll have the lamb," she decided finally.

"Lamb? I'm going for the steak."

Rochelle laughed. "Now why doesn't that surprise me? A man will always go for a steak."

He shrugged casually. "What can I say? There's nothing like a good steak. To be honest, I want to check out the taste of your organic beef here in Australia. See if it's as good as what I serve at the restaurant in my resort."

The waiter appeared and took their orders. Daniel ordered a bottle of champagne before she had a chance to say that she'd prefer not to have any alcohol. She wanted to keep a clear head.

Once the waiter left, she pulled her iPad toward her and with a few quick strokes brought up the hotel app on the screen. She pushed her tablet over the table toward Daniel.

"Here's one of the newest features we have—the Kulang Resort app. People can research all the treatments we offer. Once they've decided, they can then send an email to our bookings staff, who will enter in all the details. When the guests arrive, they receive a printout of the dates and times of their treatments."

He picked up the tablet and studied the screen. He didn't say much, and it was all she could do not to ask flat out what he thought about it. She had spent a long time with the app designers working on exactly what she wanted. The feedback she'd received thus far from the guests who had used it was extremely positive. He laid the tablet back on the table. "This is fantastic. Who came up with this idea?"

She cleared her throat. "I did. I worked with a designer, and I can honestly say it's turned out better than I expected or hoped it would."

"Did you copyright or patent this program?"

"Yes, of course."

"I would love to have this available to give to my guests. It's so innovative. This application would be a great first step in my new plans to make my resort the best in Washington State and eventually, in the United States. Damn, I wish I'd come up with this."

"I'm sure a smart guy like you can come up with a similar app."

He sent her a wicked smile. "You wouldn't be interested in helping me come up with one for my resort, would you?"

Rochelle was honored to be asked, but even though she wanted to do it, she couldn't. From the short conversation they'd shared, she got the impression Daniel's focus was on his resort and his career. Just like her.

She reached across the table and laid her hand over Daniel's to soften the blow of rejection. Like every other time they'd touched, electricity sizzled through her, starting at her fingers and ending at the tips of her toes. How would her body react if they did kiss, when a simple touch left her craving for so much more?

"Daniel, I'm really sorry, but I can't. It would be a breach of my employment contract."

He twisted his hand so that he took control of the grip. They probably looked like a couple to the other diners. When that thought hit her, she pulled her hand away. She didn't want to give anyone that impression.

"I thought that might be the case, but there was no harm in asking." He looked back down at the iPad. "I think I can work out something similar. So what else have you introduced to the resort?" he asked as he topped her champagne glass.

"I know what you're trying to do," she said on a laugh.

"Really, what's that?" He was innocence personified. She knew better.

"You're trying to get me tipsy so I'll spill some trade secrets." She pushed her champagne glass away and picked up her water glass and took a long drink. "Let me assure you, that's not going to happen."

"You can't stop me from trying." He leaned forward and beckoned her with a crook of his finger. It was as if he had a piece of invisible string between them and she found herself leaning toward him. "If I could, I would poach you for my own resort. Whisk you away, and the moment you set foot in Emerald Springs you wouldn't want to leave."

Rochelle sat back, surprised at how tempted she was by the thought of travelling to the other side of the world—travelling to a place where she wouldn't have to worry when the phone rang that it was her mother wanting more money to feed her habit. She couldn't do it, though. Couldn't take that step into the unknown. What if things didn't work out? What if she was stuck in Emerald Springs and had no way of getting home because she was dependent on Daniel Whitman?

No, that wasn't happening. She wasn't going to be dependent on anyone again. They always let her down.

She cleared her throat and this time spoke a little louder, a little stronger. "That's an extremely tempting offer, but I will have to pass. I like my job."

"Such a shame. I think you and I could be a force to be reckoned with."

Now she was intrigued. The man had only met her earlier today. They'd spent a total time of less than two hours together, and he already thought they'd make a good team?

Their meals arrived at that moment, but when the waiter left, Rochelle asked the burning question in the forefront of her mind.

"What makes you think we'll be a force to be reckoned with?"

• • •

Daniel finished his mouthful of food. Ever since she'd opened her office door and all but fell into his embrace—again, he'd been tortured with thoughts of the two of them naked, arms entwined.

He was fighting the urge now to reach across the table and pull her into his arms again. He'd never felt this sudden attraction with anyone since the day he'd discovered just how luscious girls could be. If he wanted this evening to end with both of them exploring more than just each other's minds, he needed to keep his focus above his belt buckle.

"Well, you have a lot of innovative ideas. With you on my team, Emerald Paradise would surpass even this resort as the best in the world."

"That's ambitious."

"You can't succeed in this world unless you aim for the top."

"That's true. Although I'm sure your current marketing person would be a bit upset at being replaced, especially if they're good at their job."

"Seeing as that's me at present, I'll gladly pass the job on."

He saw questions flit through her mind. If he pushed it a little more, could he lure her away from Kulang Resort all the way to Emerald Springs?

"So you're a jack-of-all-trades. Who's in charge while you're here?"

"Not quite. My marketing person just upped and left a month ago, and I haven't found the right person to replace him. Although my cousin Ashley has stepped up and helped out, I can't expect her to continue forever."

"Maybe she wants the job. Have you asked her?"

"No, I haven't. But I know she likes working at the family tea farm, and while she has innovative ideas, working at the resort on a permanent basis would stifle her creativity. She likes the freedom to move around. There's also my Uncle Sam; he's not bad at marketing, just a little old-fashioned in his ideas. But with my dad talking about retiring soon, I'm sure he'll want to retire, too. I want someone who's going to stay in the job and at the resort for a long time." Daniel raised his glass, smiling slowly at his beautiful dinner companion. "Are you sure I can't lure you away?" He wouldn't mind working with Rochelle Harris ... or having her in close proximity day in and day out. He could imagine how they'd work off the day's stresses together.

The thought pulled him up short. He wasn't looking for a long-term commitment. He wasn't looking for a relationship at all. Not to mention if they did decide to pursue a relationship and it didn't work out, she'd probably leave and he'd be back to square one again. No, best he kept their dealings professional, no matter how tempting she was. He was looking for ideas to get his resort to the top of the field, not a life partner.

Her soft laughter broke through his thoughts. "No matter what you say, you won't convince me to move. I'm very happy, and I've got lots of ideas to bring to the table." She leaned forward and he saw the look of steely determination in her eyes. "I plan on keeping Kulang Resort the world's best spa and resort for a very long time."

"That sounds like a challenge."

She gave an elegant shrug of her shoulders, causing her dress to tighten across her breasts. He clenched his hands a little tighter as they itched to trace her firm flesh. The neckline of her dress wasn't indecently low, but it was low enough to tempt him into wanting to see if she tasted as sweet as she looked.

He bit back a groan. He was acting like an adolescent teenager the first time he saw a hot girl. He was a grown man, and he'd already decided that no matter how tempting it was to pursue something with Rochelle, it wasn't a good idea. Especially if he could wear her down and steal her away from this resort. Everyone had a price. He was sure if he came across the right temptation to lure her, he would be more than happy to pay her price.

"What is life but a constant challenge?"

"Don't I know it," she muttered.

"Sounds like there's a story there."

As she looked up her blue eyes dulled, like the stormy swells of the ocean. "Doesn't everyone have a story they'd rather not remember?"

Against his better judgment, he reached out and laid his hand over hers. He expected her to pull away, like she did before. But she surprised him by leaving her hand under his. "Life sucks sometimes, doesn't it?"

This time she did pull her hand back, and he felt bereft at the loss of her skin beneath his.

"It does, but you can't change the crap that happened to you in the past. You need to move forward."

There was a wealth of bitterness in her voice, and he couldn't help but wonder what or who had put it there. Somehow over the course of eating their main meal, the conversation had turned from business to very personal. He was pretty sure Rochelle wasn't aware of what she was saying. There was a lost look about her, as if she were miles away and not a few feet across a dinner table from him.

He wanted to bring back that smile. The smile that lit up her soul.

"Do you want anything else?" he asked and nodded toward her empty plate.

"No, thank you, how about you?"

"I'm good, but there is something I would like to do." Daniel leaned forward, aiming to bring back that spark of competitive fire in her blue eyes.

"What would you like to do?"

His mind shot off in a multitude of different directions as she took the bait. Most of it was not dinner conversation. Luckily, they were finished.

He lowered his voice. "There's a lot I'd like to do with you, Rochelle."

Even in the candlelight he could see the telltale flush of pink bloom rush into her cheeks.

"But, I'll settle for a walk around the gardens," he continued. "If you're interested."

God, he hoped she'd say yes.

• • •

Rochelle didn't trust herself or her professional reputation alone in the darkened gardens with him, but she found herself nodding her head. Her tongue seemed glued to the top of her mouth. She picked up her glass of water and took a sip. "We can do that, if you like. Although I don't think you're going to see too much. We don't generally light the gardens. We wanted to keep the surrounding rainforest as natural as possible so we didn't upset the nocturnal animals."

Daniel's response was to stand and hold out his hand for her. It would seem rude if she didn't take it. She stood and placed her hand in his.

"I'm sure that whatever light you have will be enough for me."

"It's a fine evening, so we'll have the moonlight to guide us, too."

"Do you want to drop your stuff back at your office?" he asked as they started toward the exit.

"Yes, that makes sense."

After the quick stop, they were in the garden ten minutes later. Rochelle wasn't too sure of what he wanted to see, but she led him to the lake in the middle of the relaxation garden.

They sat quietly on one of the benches overlooking the lake. The only sound was the insects as they sang their evening songs. The trees whispered softly in harmony as a gentle breeze ruffled through their leaves.

On many occasions when she needed a timeout from the stresses of work, she came here and let the wonder of Mother Nature surround and hold her. Looking at the trees that had weathered many things and still stood the test of time always made her realize her problems were nothing in comparison to what rainforests around the world faced due to the endless and senseless clearing of land, all in the name of progress. She was glad no one could touch this pristine forest, and she hoped it remained that way.

"This reminds me of home," Daniel whispered beside her. She'd been so lost in her thoughts, she'd almost forgotten he was with her. His words held a world of feeling. He continued to surprise her. There was more to Daniel Whitman than merely being a resort owner. He was a man who was connected to his home in a way she could never understand. Living at Kulang was the longest time she'd spent in one house after her father died.

"What about it is similar?"

"We have a lake in the middle of my resort that is almost a mirror image of this one. I've never found the peace and harmony I find sitting beside it anywhere, except here. I could just sit for hours and forget my troubles."

"I feel the same; there's something so peaceful about sitting by the lake."

"My mom and I used to have lots of conversations by the lake. I shared so many secrets with her and the lake."

"She sounds like a great mother. I would like to meet her one day." Rochelle could hear the wistfulness and bitterness in her voice. What would it be like to have a mother who didn't rip you off when the first opportunity arose? A mother who nurtured and cared for you, more than she cared about what the next deal of a card from a croupier could mean for her future. A mother who didn't drive her husband to an early grave with her gambling habit.

"You can't," he whispered the words. As he lifted his head to look at the stars she thought she glimpsed the sheen of tears in his eyes. Yes, there was so much more to Daniel than she first assumed.

He cleared his throat and lowered his head to look back at the lake. "She would've liked to have met you, too. You both would've gotten on well. And she would have loved this resort. I wish I could've shared it with her."

"I'm sorry," Rochelle said quietly. He spoke of her with such reverence and love. She reached out and laid her hand over his. "How long ago did she pass away?"

"Five years ago. She had breast cancer. She beat it once, but the second time it sunk its claws in deeper, and there was nothing we could do for her."

She wanted to reach up and touch his cheek. Soothe the lines of despair the moonlight highlighted.

"Cancer is awful." Her words sounded hollow, and she wished she could take them back.

"It is, but no matter how much pain she was in, she always had time for me. She always knew when things were getting to me. She'd take me by the hand and say, 'Walk with me. ' Even if I didn't want to say anything, she managed to pry it out of me. Usually when we were sitting by the lake." He gave a chuckle. "Even now I'm saying things I've never told anyone. My brothers don't know how often mom and I would walk to the lake. Maybe there's power in water after all."

Rochelle felt honored that he chose to share something so special with her. A person he'd met only a few hours ago. "It could be the water making you feel closer to her spirit. Do you still sit by the lake when you need to think?"

Moments passed and she didn't think he was going to answer. She risked a glance at him and saw pain and sadness in his face as he sat gazing at the water. He seemed so far away, even though he was sitting right beside her. She ached to touch him. To let him know that he wasn't alone.

As if sensing her scrutiny, he turned to her. "I don't go to the lake anymore. It hurts too much," he finished on a whisper.

Before she could talk herself out of it, she leaned forward and laid a soft kiss on his lips. They were firm and inviting and the urge to deepen the kiss was strong. Reluctantly she pulled away. "I'm sorry for bringing you to our lake."

Rochelle started to move to her right, but Daniel reached out and gently held her head in both his hands.

"You have no reason to be sorry. I'm glad you brought me here."

In the moonlight, she saw his lips curl into a small smile. "And I hope you won't be mad at me when I do this."

She had no time to react to his words before his warm lips took possession of hers again. All rational thought left her mind, and she let the sensation of Daniel's lips moving over hers rush through her. Her arms wound up and around his neck, and she scooted along the bench a little closer to him. She opened her mouth and he deepened the kiss, moaning into the night. His hands roved over her back before moving to the sides and up until his fingers brushed the underside of her breast. A million darts of pleasure spiked through her. Her nipples puckered and pushed against her satin bra. She wanted him to touch her right there under the moonlight in front of a lake that signified special memories for him. She pushed her chest forward, encouraging him to touch her. The ability to be sensible had flown out of her mind the moment he started kissing her.

"Chelle," he breathed against her lips. "You feel so good."

His words weren't crude, but they were enough to bring her back to the present. Back to remembering she was in an area where anybody could observe them together. Any member of staff could see her associating with a guest. What had she been thinking?

She pulled back and put some distance between them on the bench. She tried to catch her breath after the most amazing kiss she'd ever experienced. As she brought her fingers up to her mouth, she saw that her hand was trembling.

"We shouldn't have done that, Daniel."

Chapter 4

Rochelle picked up the piece of paper, trying again to decipher the words in front of her. The document was explaining a fascinating technique of using gongs and crystal singing bowls as a way of encouraging meditation and relaxation in people suffering from serious and life-threatening illnesses, in an effort to encourage the body to a state of well-being where it can slow down the progress of the disease. She was trying to convince her bosses that they should look at bringing a facility like this to the resort. It would work well with their existing spa treatments.

Instead of focusing on work, however, all she could think about was the kiss she and Daniel had shared last night. Every time she closed her eyes, she could feel his lips on hers, their firmness lightly caressing then deepening, until all rational thought left her.

A knock on her door brought her out of her thoughts of Daniel Whitman. He was a danger to her goals. For the sake of her sanity, she needed to stay well away from him.

"Come in," she called and closed the file. Until she had a concrete proposal put together to present to the board, she didn't want anyone knowing about her plan.

Her assistant, Melanie, walked in.

"What's up, Mel?"

Melanie closed the door and a sense of dread filtered through her like water streaking down a window on a rainy day. Melanie never closed the door when she came into the office.

Rochelle sat a little straighter. "Has there been an accident? Is a guest hurt?"

As Melanie laughed, she relaxed a little. "No, nothing like that, but it does involve a guest."

"O-kayy," Rochelle drew out the word.

"Daniel Whitman is here to see you again. I tried to tell him that you were busy and weren't seeing anyone, but he was insistent." As Melanie lowered her voice, Rochelle's sense of dread returned. "He said he had dinner with you last night. Is that true?"

Even though everything in her wanted her to lie to her assistant, she couldn't. "Yes, I did. What does Mr. Whitman want?"

"I can't believe you had dinner with him. He's gorgeous. I wish a hunk of a man like him would ask me out."

Even though she totally agreed with her assessment of Daniel, Rochelle couldn't let Melanie know that.

"It was a pleasant evening. So what does he want?" She hoped by asking the question again, Melanie would get her focus back on track—the reason for Daniel's visit.

As if Melanie realized she'd taken her curiosity a little far, she cleared her throat. "He said he wanted a tour of the resort."

Rochelle nodded her head. How was she going to get around having to take Daniel on a tour? It was part of her job, and one she normally enjoyed. But having to walk side by side with the man who rocked her world with one little kiss was something she didn't think she could do.

She glanced down at the folder on her desk and her get-out-of-jail-free card presented itself to her. If she wanted to get this new proposal ready for the upcoming board meeting, she needed to do more research into Resonances, the facility she had identified.

"Look, can you show him around for me, Melanie? I'm working on this new project, and since I have to contact the lady who runs this facility in a few minutes, it would be a great help if you could do this for me."

"Sure." Enthusiasm was leaping from her every pore. It was clear her assistant didn't mind the chore at all.

"Great." Rochelle picked up the piece of paper to indicate that for her, the matter was closed. She tried to ignore the stab in her chest at the thought of Daniel flirting with Melanie.

She whooshed out a breath as her door closed; hopefully, now that she knew Daniel wouldn't be bothering her, she could get on with her plans for Kulang Resort's future and her career—the only thing she had control over.

She tried not to think about Melanie and Daniel strolling around the resort, and Daniel teasing a smile out of her assistant. It shouldn't matter what they did; just because she and Daniel had shared a kiss last night, it didn't give her any control over the man.

Rochelle had no doubt that when it came to the business side of the tour, her assistant was more than capable of dealing with any questions he might have.

She dived for the phone when it rang, glad for the distraction. "Rochelle Harris."

"Good morning, Ms. Harris, how are you?"

She sat a little straighter when she heard the chairman of the board of directors' voice. "I'm well, thank you, sir. How are you?"

"Good. I wanted to talk to you about this new vibration treatment center proposal you emailed me. I've spoken to other members of the board and they expressed definite interest. Can you give me some more details?"

Excitement bubbled through her.

She spent the next fifteen minutes explaining everything she'd learned so far to the chairman, including her plan to call the director of Resonances to find out more about the medical services they offered.

When the call was finished, Rochelle got the green light to present her proposal to the board at the next meeting in two weeks.

As she let the buzz of the phone call flow through her, her mind ticked off everything she needed to accomplish in the next two weeks. The board meeting was going to be the biggest one in her career. She couldn't afford to let herself be sidetracked. And there was no time like right now to tackle the challenge.

She picked up her phone again and placed a call to the Resonances's director, hoping the woman was willing to enter into a partnership with the resort. The move would be just as beneficial for her as it was for Kulang … and Rochelle.

All thoughts of Daniel and Melanie on their tour were a million miles away.

• • •

Daniel smiled as Melanie waxed lyrical about the treatments the spa offered. There were a couple of new techniques he could take back, but nothing outstanding that would set Emerald Springs apart from the rest. He wanted something innovative and unique, something that none of the resorts in the United States had ever seen. He had really hoped Kulang Resort would have something he could use. They were one of the most profitable resorts in Australia, booked out months in advance. He'd only gotten a room due to a last-minute cancellation. He'd used that as a sign this trip was going to be fruitful for him. The last thing he wanted was to return to Emerald Springs and face his father and Adam with nothing to show but an expensive plane flight and accommodation bill, proving that for the first time in his business life, he'd gone off on a trip without fully researching every detail. The impulsiveness to take this trip stemmed from seeing everyone around him falling in love. Seeing his father and Patty together blurred his sensibilities. He could've waited for emails from Rochelle and gotten his questions answered that way. He didn't need to have taken this trip. For the first time ever, he'd let a situation get the better of him and he'd run.

A hand landed on his forearm. "Is there something wrong?"

Melanie's breathy tone was starting to get to him. Every action seemed to be suggestive. Normally he'd engage and even flirt a little, but today, he just couldn't be bothered. He didn't want to be walking around the resort with Melanie. He wanted Rochelle by his side. It was her elusive, sweet scent he wanted filling his nostrils, not Melanie's cloying, musky perfume, which even overpowered the scent of the essential oils burning throughout the spa.

"Daniel, is there something wrong?" This time her tone was sharper, and he realized he'd not answered her. Her hand was still on his arm so he rested his own hand lightly over hers.

"No, everything's fine." He had to come up with a reasonable explanation for his vagueness. "I'm taking in the spa's ambiance. It's very relaxing, and I can see why it's popular with everyone."

Her smile broadened. "Yes, we're very proud of it, and Rochelle always makes sure we have the most innovative techniques to tempt and relax our guests."

"She works hard, doesn't she?" he asked, hoping to get a bit more of an insight into the woman he'd not been able to forget since experiencing the most amazing kiss with her.

"Yes, she does; she's completely focused on her job. Doesn't let anything or anyone sway her from her goals."

It sounded like Rochelle was as chained to a desk as he was. It gave him a little hope that he wouldn't have to compete with another man for her time. She hadn't pulled away from him last night when they'd kissed; in fact, she'd melted into his touch. Then he remembered her parting words and hoped they hadn't meant there was someone in her life.

"She's been at the resort for a long time, hasn't she?" he asked as they headed out of the spa facility and into the gardens surrounding it.

"Yes, she's worked hard to get to the position she's in today."

Daniel knew he shouldn't ask Melanie about Rochelle. But his interest was piqued, and he had a feeling Rochelle may not be forthcoming with information. It was sneaky, but he wasn't above using the charm he'd decided to skip earlier to get what he wanted now. He might even find out if there is a man in Rochelle's life.

"Do you know what she did before the resort?"

"Well, she initially started out as a massage therapist in a salon in Brisbane. She never said why, but she had to leave school at fifteen. She worked during the day and studied for her marketing degree in the evening. Then when she finished her studies, she received an internship at the resort and worked her way to marketing manager. Since she's been in that position, the resort's reputation has grown in leaps and bounds. She doesn't like to talk about it much, and I'm probably sounding like a fan girl, but I respect Rochelle so much. She's a great boss to work for. In her first year as marketing manager, the resort was awarded the prestigious HM Award for the best resort in Australia."

Daniel's respect for Rochelle grew a little more. He'd known she was good at her job, but the fact she'd worked and studied at the same time impressed him to no end. He also tried not to dwell on Melanie mentioning that Rochelle had been a massage therapist. He wouldn't mind letting Rochelle's hands massage the tension out of his shoulders. His body hardened at the thought of him returning the favor.

"Here we are, the Rose Garden." This time, he was grateful for the interruption. His thoughts were starting to go X-rated, and he didn't want to give Melanie the impression that she was the one getting him hot.

But just his luck, a few feet away by the rose covered arch, stood the woman he'd been thinking about, clipboard in hand, seemingly taking notes. As if sensing his perusal, she turned her head and glanced over her shoulder. He could tell the moment she realized it was him she was looking at. Her eyes widened and her tongue darted out to moisten her lips. He recognized the action for what it was—she hadn't expected to see him and it unnerved her. As her eyes darted between him and Melanie and how close they stood together, he could almost swear she was jealous. Her head flicked back to her clipboard.

Interesting.

He decided to test his theory and suddenly turned to Melanie. "So, my sweet Melanie, what special things can you tell me about the Rose Garden?"

He'd raised his voice enough so that it carried toward Rochelle. Her straightening back told him everything he needed to know— she'd heard him.

Melanie played her part by giggling loudly. "Oh, Daniel, there's nothing special about the garden, apart from using the rose petals in the potpourri that is placed in every resort room. And one of the local residents extracts the rose oil from the plants for the essential oils we sell."

He risked a glance in Rochelle's direction and noticed that she had moved a little closer to their conversation.

"It's a very romantic atmosphere," he commented lightly. "Do you hold many weddings here?"

"No, the resort doesn't hold weddings here," said a husky voice—a voice he wanted to hear moan his name.

Daniel bit back the grin that threatened to stretch over his face. Rochelle had joined the conversation—just as he wanted.

"Good morning, Ms. Harris." He went for formal, hoping to irritate her a little. Her eyes flashed blue flame as they narrowed at his words and tone. An answering fire started deep in his belly. He wanted to see what those eyes would say when in the throes of passion. He clenched his fists to stop from reaching out and taking her in his arms.

"Good morning, Mr. Whitman. I hope Melanie is answering all your questions about the services we offer?"

"Yes, she's been more than helpful." He glanced sideways at Melanie. "Haven't you?"

Melanie blushed, and he felt badly for leading her on with the express intention of making Rochelle jealous.

"Well that's great, I'll leave you to it."

Before he had a chance to stop her, Rochelle turned and marched away. Her back was rigid, and if she'd been on hard ground, he was sure he would've been able to hear her shoes stomp on the pavement.

He sighed and ran a hand through his hair. This wasn't how he had wanted things to turn out when he'd shown up at the resort's management offices this morning.

"Do you want to go get a coffee, Daniel? I can call you Daniel, can't I?" Melanie asked.

His desire to annoy Rochelle had now created a sticky situation. His brothers had always called him out for thinking only of the end result and not others when his focus was on a single goal— and today that goal had been to get Rochelle's attention.

"I don't think that would be a good idea. You know I'm a guest and you are part of the staff." He started off gently, hoping to let her down lightly.

"Not a problem—it's not really against the rules for staff to mingle with the guests."

Now that was interesting. Last night Rochelle had intimated that the management of the hotel didn't take too kindly to guests and staff members socializing. Yet Melanie was saying the exact opposite.

This was an important piece of information he could use to his advantage. The way Rochelle responded to his kiss was not the reaction of a person who was indifferent to his touch.

He couldn't do anything about pursuing Rochelle until he'd sorted out this mess he'd found himself in.

"Still, I think it would be best if we don't have a coffee. I'm here on business and have a lot of things to cover in a short amount of time. How about I walk you back to your office?"

Her smile slipped and disappointment filled her eyes. He was a complete jerk.

"Sure, okay," Melanie said.

As they made their way back to the offices, Daniel supposed the next thing he could explore would be Kulang's operations with regard to being eco-friendly. He was sure Adam had a good handle on that topic. After all, it was what he did for Eco Initiatives before leaving his L.A. office to run Emerald Tea Farm. But this resort was located in the middle of a heritage-listed rainforest as opposed to Emerald Paradise's privately owned land. Surely Kulang had to use different methods to comply with those regulations and maintain its five-star green rating.

The thought of work didn't excite him. The thought of Rochelle did, though. He needed to get her away from her comfort zone— the resort—to a place where there would be no chance of their conversation being overheard. Then he could find out why she'd tried to use a no-fraternization policy on him. His problem was he had no means to leave the resort. He could check with the concierge and see if there was a hotel car he could use to whisk her away. He would bet Emerald Paradise that she wouldn't want a resort driver taking them to whatever location he settled on. Or, he could find out where the best restaurant in close proximity to the resort was and take her there. Perhaps away from the resort she would let her guard down and he could find the true Rochelle. Or perhaps once she was away from what was comfortable, she would clam up.

He was in a situation where he didn't know which way to turn, and confusion wasn't a position he was used to. Instinct made him open the door before Melanie could do it when they reached the suite of resort offices.

"Thanks again for the great tour, Melanie. You've been more than helpful."

As the assistant took her seat at her desk, he could sense her reserve, her previously relaxed manner completely gone. "It was a pleasure, Mr. Whitman. If you need any more help or have any questions, I'll be happy to assist you."

"Do you think you could check with Ms. Harris to see if she has a couple of minutes to spare?"

He hadn't planned on speaking to Rochelle so soon after their encounter in the garden, but because she was only a closed door away from him, the urge to see her was strong.

"I'll check."

•••

Rochelle could hear the low tones of voices in the outer office. Melanie and Daniel had returned. Were they making plans for dinner that evening? Would he kiss Melanie the way he'd kissed her? Had he only been feeding her a line last night when he'd shared his inner thoughts about his mother?

God, she hated the way Daniel was making her feel. They'd shared one dinner, a business dinner at that. It shouldn't matter what he did. He was only here for a few days. She had to remember that.

A short knock sounded on her door. "Come in."

She looked up and Melanie poked her head around the door. "Mr. Whitman was wondering if you had a couple of minutes to spare."

The best answer was to deny his request. In the garden, she'd wanted to march over there and rip his hand off her assistant's arm. But Rochelle also knew if she didn't see him and then found out that he'd left the resort, she would be angry with herself. And a part of her wanted to see him.

"Yes, that should be fine." But something in Melanie's features wasn't quite right. Rochelle got up from her chair and walked over to her assistant. "Is everything okay, Mel?"

The woman nodded. "I'll send him in."

Before Rochelle could stop her, Melanie whirled away and told Daniel that she would see him. The anger she had tempered flared to life again. Clearly, Daniel had upset Melanie, and she would find out what he'd done.

"Thanks for seeing me." His smooth American accent flowed over her like water over rocks. "I wanted to…"

"Wait, don't say a word." Rochelle closed the door and strode over to her desk. She pressed a button as she picked up her phone. "Melanie, I need you to run over to the gift shop and pick up some of that Emu Oil Face Cream. I want to package it for a guest."

That should get Melanie out of the office while she had a go at Daniel for upsetting her assistant. When she was sure the woman was out of earshot, she rounded her desk and stood in front of Daniel. His spicy aftershave wafted toward her, reminding her of their encounter at the lake the previous evening. Her body softened and she almost swayed toward him.

"What did you do to upset Melanie?"

The shocked look on his face told her that wasn't what he'd been expecting to come out of her.

"I didn't do anything."

Rochelle arched her brow. She could see the telltale hint of red on his cheeks.

"Fine, I may have flirted a little with her, but in my defense, she flirted with me first."

"Clearly you did more than flirt, Daniel. I know my assistant and she is upset."

"I may have used her to make you jealous."

The admission took the wind out of her sails. What could she say? That it worked? That she wanted to scratch her assistant's eyes out? She couldn't say any of that to him. The idea that after one dinner and one kiss, they could both feel so strongly about each other shocked her.

It was wrong. Wrong. Wrong. Wrong.

She couldn't feel this way about a man so soon.

The silence dragged between them and Rochelle knew she had to say something before it became even more uncomfortable.

"I don't quite know what to say to that."

He laughed and an answering smile tugged at the corners of her mouth.

"I don't think there's much to say." He shook his head as if to dislodge or organize his thoughts. "I can't quite believe I said it either." The words were spoken softly and she wondered whether she'd imagined them.

Deciding that the dark, murky waters of jealousy were something she didn't want to dive into, she changed tack. "So, okay. Melanie said you wanted to see me. Was there something specific you wanted to talk about?"

"No, nothing specific but I would really like you to show me the facilities. Melanie did a great job and explained a lot of things. But you're the marketing manager. I want to know how you bring in the exclusive clientele. I want to attract A-list people to my resort. I want to change the face of Emerald Springs. I need your help."

Rochelle was speechless. Standing before her was a man who ran a resort so far away, it was a different day there. He dressed like he owned the world, and he was asking her for her marketing advice and help? Surely he could employ someone who would be able to generate the type of business he wanted to attract. He'd just been flirting with her last night when he'd told her he wanted her to work for him, hadn't he? There was no way he could've been serious about hiring her. No way at all. "Don't you have your own staff to help you with that?"

She stood her ground as Daniel strode toward her, purpose in every step. He took hold of her hands, and the heat from them traversed up her arms, warming her where she didn't realize she was cold.

"I told you I'm short a marketing manager at present. But that's beside the point. Rochelle, I came here because of Kulang's reputation. You're responsible for that. I came here because of you."

Chapter 5

The knock Rochelle had been dreading sounded on her door. Daniel had been insistent on wanting to have another meeting with her, and she hadn't been able to put him off. He'd backed her into a corner. He'd come to Kulang seeking her professional opinion. To be sought out in that manner was a dream come true. If only it wasn't packaged in a man who had the flirty side of her wanting to get to know him better.

She closed the door on those thoughts. He was a rival. He could be using her just like Justin had. Keep it all about the business basics, she cautioned herself. Whatever happened, she couldn't mention her idea about Resonances and bringing a similar facility to Kulang. It would be devastating to her to lose those plans.

She could do this. "Come in."

The door opened but she wasn't prepared for the Daniel standing in her doorway. She'd expected the corporate Daniel; instead, she got the casual, sexy Daniel, and he was far more dangerous for her hormones. He'd changed from his suit into a tight fitting white t-shirt and faded blue jeans.

She was in so much trouble.

Rochelle took a couple of deep breaths to get her emotions and thoughts under control. There was no way she could let him know how much his presence was starting to affect her. She had to stop letting him get to her. For goodness sake they'd only met the day before.

"Good afternoon, Daniel." Rochelle stood and smoothed down her skirt. "Are you ready for your second tour?"

He laughed and held out his hand for her. She hesitated for a moment before placing her hand in his. "I cannot wait for your insight, my lovely Rochelle." He finished by raising her hand to his lips and placed a soft kiss on the top of her palm. Her knees weakened at the charming gesture, the warm imprint of his lips brushing her skin etched in her mind. Disappointment filled her when he let it go. She should've been grateful—the last thing she needed was for Melanie to see them walk out hand in hand, especially after Daniel had been flirting with the other woman, too. "Mel, I'm thinking I'll be gone for a while, but if there's anything urgent that comes up, I have my mobile so just give me a call," she said in passing.

"Sure, Rochelle."

"Can you give me a minute?" Daniel's question came out of the blue and she didn't know what he was up to when he stopped at Melanie's desk. "Melanie, I'd like to apologize for my behavior earlier today. It was inappropriate, and I'm sorry if I misled or upset you. It definitely wasn't my intention."

With those few words, Rochelle fell a little deeper under his spell. He truly sounded remorseful for upsetting Melanie, and for him to apologize was extremely gentlemanly.

"Thank you," her assistant whispered, clearly as shocked as Rochelle was by Daniel's actions.

"Shall we?" he asked as he joined her at the door.

Rochelle was incapable of speech, so she just nodded.

They walked quietly down the hallway. "That was really nice of you to apologize to Melanie."

"It was the least I could do. My brothers are always telling me that I can be a complete jerk sometimes. Melanie was doing her job, and even though she did initially flirt with me, I shouldn't have given her any reason to think there was any interest on my part when there wasn't."

"Well I'm glad you did it." Wanting to get off that sensitive subject, she grasped onto the one thing that she guessed would be a safe subject to talk about. "So how many brothers do you have?"

"Two: one older and one younger."

Being an only child, Rochelle had often wondered what would've happened if she'd had a sibling. Would her mother have fallen into her gambling habit? If her mother hadn't, would her father still be alive today? Where would she be now if her father had lived?

But indulging in *what ifs* was a waste of mental energy. Her life was what it was meant to be. All her struggles growing up, trying to keep a roof over her and her mother's head while she worked at the crappy beauty salon giving facials and massages to people who treated her like crap were what defined her and gave her the determination to get on the career path she was on. After their fifth landlord in as many months had suggested he'd turn a blind eye to the missing rent if Rochelle came to his apartment later that night, Rochelle had packed her bags and walked away. It had been two years after that before she'd spoken to her mother again, but nothing had changed. It had now been five years since she'd last spoken to her and seen her face to face.

The success she had made of her life was due to her own tenacity, not her mother's.

"Hey, where did you go?"

Rochelle blinked a couple of times. "Sorry, just thinking about—ahh it doesn't matter. You were telling me about your brothers?"

There were some things she didn't share with people and her mother was one. Even Melanie didn't know about her past.

"I don't believe you really want to know about my brothers."

"Yes, I do," she asserted, wanting to know more about the man walking beside her. "I bet you three gave your mum a hard time growing up."

He chuckled. "Yeah, we did, but all it took was one look from Mom and we quickly stopped what we were doing."

Rochelle had an image of Daniel and his brothers as three young boys covered in mud and scrapes, each of them elbowing the other. She'd never thought about having children. Besides, what sort of mother would she make? Her own mother hadn't set a stellar example.

"I bet all you had to do was smile and she would forgive you."

"That pretty much sums up my younger brother. Chad would give Mom his cheeky, I-didn't-do-it smile and she would go easy on him. Adam and I usually got blamed because we were older. Of course, after my brothers were gone, Mom would always pull me into a hug, tell me she knew Chad had probably started it, then give me a kiss and hand me a freshly baked cookie."

Rochelle saw that Daniel's eyes were staring off in the distance, seeing not the beautiful scenery but his mum hugging him again. She hadn't realized they'd stopped walking, but they were standing in front of the spa. Part of her wanted to continue the conversation. She wanted to hear all about what he and his brothers did as boys. She also had a feeling his mother was at the center of most of those memories.

"Sounds like your mum was a smart woman." She held open the spa door. "Shall we start the tour?"

"Yep, let's go."

• • •

Daniel walked past Rochelle into the quiet ambience of the spa. He didn't know what it was about her, but he always found himself talking to her about his mom. He'd never said much to anyone about Sheila Whitman. After her death, he hadn't wanted to talk about her, not even to Chad or Adam. It hurt too much. He had been the one at her bedside when their mother died. His father had just stepped out of the room, leaving Daniel alone there.

He didn't want to think about that day. Didn't want to see the moment his mom had smiled at him one last time, told him she loved him and then closed her eyes forever.

"Daniel, is everything okay?"

He grasped at Rochelle's voice like a lifeline saving him from drowning in his memories. *Focus, man.* He was here for business, not to think about his mother.

"Yep, everything's fine. Tell me how the spa works. What happens when you arrive?"

He could see Rochelle didn't quite believe him, and he appreciated it when she didn't push him to talk more.

"Well when you arrive at the spa, you get checked in. We like to get as many details as we can get from the guests so that when they visit the resort again, and they always do, we have everything we need. We also email them *specials* flyers. This is to remind them they can order any of the creams or oils used during their treatments and have them delivered to their own homes."

"Do you have a positive open rate on the sale emails? Do you see an influx of orders after you've run a campaign? How often do you run the specials and for how long? A week? A month?"

Daniel fired the questions at her. Here was businessman Daniel. "We run bi-monthly sales. They generally last for a week and our open rate is close to thirty-five percent. The days after the initial email blast, our online sales increase by eighty-five percent."

"Those are some impressive numbers."

"Thanks. We're aiming to get to fifty percent open rate by the end of the year. When guests make their booking, most will choose an array of treatments. Armed with this advance knowledge, we space the treatments over the length of their stay so our guests can enjoy some of the other features of the resort and become attached to them as well. We make sure their last treatment is given a couple of hours before they leave the resort so they're relaxed for their journey home. As an added bonus, we have gift wrapped, airport approved sized samples of the oils or creams used during their last treatment so they can tuck them into their overnight bag. They love it. This small gesture guarantees customer satisfaction, and more importantly, repeat bookings. Nine times out of ten people are accessing the app to make another reservation on their way to the airport."

He knew by getting Rochelle to show him around the facilities he would find out much more than he had from Melanie. His first tour hadn't included the check-in procedure or the extended services they provided after the clients left.

The higher end clients he hoped to attract would appreciate that bit of extra customer service. He also liked the idea of finding out the treatments the guests wanted before they arrived—it improved the chances of upselling them at check-in.

"I like your ideas. Such simple but effective techniques."

"Everyone likes to feel they're important, and personalizing their stay and having everything ready for them when they arrive makes our guests feel unique."

"Do you get any high profile guests staying here? That's what I want to encourage at Emerald Paradise. I want a safe haven for celebrities, away from the paparazzi, where they can relax and spend time with their families in peace."

"We currently have an Oscar-winning actor and his family here. As well as a well-known Australian country and western singer. We pride ourselves on being discreet. Our staff members are put through an extensive screening process. We don't want any photos or gossip being leaked."

"That will be something I'll have to think about. Although I'm confident our staff will be discreet."

"Did Melanie take you through our treatment rooms?"

" A couple, but a lot were in use."

Rochelle glanced at her watch. "It's close to the end of the day, so most of the treatments will be finished now."

"Lead on." Daniel followed through the hallway where the muted earth tones provided a soothing atmosphere. There were intricate paintings of yellow, white, red, orange, and brown circles on the walls, subtle but effective. He didn't recognize the painting technique at all; the pattern was mesmerizing and spiritual at the same time. "What are these paintings?"

"It's a traditional Aboriginal art technique called dot painting. It's amazing watching the locals bring the artwork to life. We've only just added these paintings."

"They're beautiful." He lowered his tone; by speaking loudly, he'd disturb the atmosphere of the spa.

"We're pleased with how they turned out. We want to embrace the culture of the indigenous people of Australia. They've performed smoking ceremonies as well as corroborees at the resort. It's quite magical to see them dance. There is something about the sound of the didgeridoo that touches deep in a person's soul."

"I would love to see one."

"Unfortunately, we don't have anything planned for awhile, but it is something everyone has to experience in their life."

"That will give me an excuse to come back and see you."

The moment he uttered those words, he knew they were true. There was something about Rochelle that touched him in a way that no other woman had in a long time, if at all. Her passion for Kulang matched his own passion for Emerald Paradise. He enjoyed the conversations they'd shared. Her intellect matched her beauty and it was intoxicating. He wanted more.

Would she be open to exploring the chemistry between them? He knew she felt an attraction for him. He'd seen the way her eyes flashed with jealousy when he'd flirted with Melanie in the garden. The way Rochelle had softened toward him when he apologized to Melanie for his behavior. She wasn't immune to him. If he were to take her in his arms and kiss her, she wouldn't resist. In fact, he could guarantee she would enjoy every touch of their lips as much as he would.

"We always like to have return customers."

He laughed at her diplomatic reply. "Always the marketer," he teased.

She joined in with his laughter. "Yes, always. Now let's continue with the tour, shall we?"

"Lead on, I'll follow you anywhere."

He spent the next fifteen minutes following Rochelle around the facility. He was interested to hear how they incorporated tea into a few of their treatments. He knew the spa at Emerald Paradise did the same, but he was sure there were techniques they could learn from each other. And he definitely was going to expand the size of his spa. Kulang's facility was at least three times the size of his and each room was always booked.

"Here is one of our massage rooms."

At the mention of massage, Daniel's attention returned fully to Rochelle. Once again, a feeling of calm stole over his body. Even the most stressed person would feel some tension seep away the moment they walked into this room, due in a large part, no doubt, to the oil burning in the electric diffuser positioned near the massage table.

"I see why everyone books multiple massages. The oil teases your senses but is no way overpowering. What is the blend?"

"I'm glad you like it. The blend, I believe, is a combination of neroli and vanilla essential oils. When used together they give the client a sense of bliss where they focus on themselves and leave all thoughts of career and other world stresses behind."

He found his gaze tracking back to the massage table. He wondered if he could talk Rochelle into giving him a massage. His body stirred at the thought of her hands on him.

"So Melanie was telling me that you used to be a massage therapist." He turned and looked at Rochelle, who was still standing by the door. "Do you still give massages?"

Please, God let her say yes.

• • •

Daniel's question burned in her brain as she flexed her fingers, a reflexive action to loosen them up before she started a massage. Her eyes darted to the table, closing as she envisioned Daniel lying face down with a snowy white towel draped over his ass: his muscles rippling beneath her oily fingers as she kneaded the tension out of him; his skin warm and soft; little moans of delight coming from him as her fingers worked their magic then drifted underneath the towel to massage his butt, knowing it would be as firm as his back; Daniel rolling over and taking her in his arms and kissing her, their lips meeting in a kiss that took her breath away; his hands doing an exploration of their own all over her body . . .

"Chelle?"

Her eyes snapped open and connected with Daniel's. She hoped her eyes weren't mirroring what she'd been imagining. She stepped back a pace, increasing the distance between them. Trying to calm herself she breathed deeply, the scent from the oils filling her senses. The blend in the burner wasn't an aphrodisiac of any sort, but her body had been burning slowly with the desire to have Daniel hold her again.

She had to stop these thoughts. He was just passing through. There was no hope of a relationship between them. "Sometimes, but I don't massage guests."

Daniel started to move toward her, his steps by no means threatening. To anyone looking at them it would seem casual, but she felt glued to the spot. In truth, she didn't want to move away from him.

He reached past her and closed the door, effectively trapping them inside. His body heat reached out to her and she swayed a little closer in answer. "Maybe I'll have to see if I can change your mind."

She took a step back, then another. With every step she took, Daniel advanced toward her. The backs of her thighs hit the massage table. She had nowhere else to go.

"What are you doing, Daniel?"

His hand went to rub his right shoulder, stretching his T-shirt tight across his chest. "I find that I'm in need of a shoulder rub."

Rochelle clenched her hands. "Well we could make an appointment for you to receive a massage tomorrow. I can make sure you have our best masseuse."

"That won't do at all."

"Why not? Most guests would be delighted to be given that opportunity."

"Ahh but I'm not your typical guest, and besides, I believe the best masseuse here at Kulang is standing right in front of me." He reached out and trailed a finger down her cheek. "Please, Rochelle."

His gentle touch frazzled her brain and all sensible and rational thought went out the window. "Okay."

Before she had time to snatch back the word, Daniel had taken a couple of steps back, pulling his t-shirt off. His hand went to the buckle of his belt.

"Wait," she all but yelled the word to him.

"What?"

"I'm giving you a shoulder rub not a full massage; you can keep your jeans on."

Rochelle didn't trust the glint of mischief lighting the depths of his eyes. "Is that right?" His hands went to work on his belt. "I think I'll be more comfortable without my jeans on."

She could argue the point. Or she could walk out and leave him without laying a finger on him. Instead, she turned around and walked to where the towels were neatly folded on the warming shelves.

I can do this. I can do this. She chanted in her mind. It wasn't as if she'd never massaged a man before. She'd massaged plenty and good-looking ones, too. But this was Daniel. A man she found herself extremely attracted to. She'd never been attracted to a client before.

"Are you going to give that towel to me?"

She whirled around, making sure she kept her gaze on his face. All the while thinking: *Don't look down. Don't look down.* "Here you go," she said holding out the towel. "Why don't you lie down and I'll get the oils ready."

She brushed past him and went over to the table that had an array of oils lined up. She poured some base oil into a bowl then added some neroli, cedarwood and lavender. She swirled the bowl to mix the oils.

"What is the blend you're using?" Daniel asked.

"It's a 'stress-buster' blend. The shoulders are an area which hold a lot of the body's stresses. This blend, combined with the massage, will help release the tension, and you should feel lighter in spirit."

Rochelle placed the bowl on the small table tucked underneath the massage bed. She flexed her fingers to loosen them and rolled her head, in her own attempt to relax her tight neck muscles.

"Are you ready?"

"More ready than you'll ever know, Chelle."

Choosing to ignore the double meaning of Daniel's words, Rochelle reached for the bowl and poured a small amount into her hands, rubbing them to warm the oil.

She laid her hands in the middle of his shoulder blades, resting them there for a moment. Her fingers tingled at the point of contact with Daniel's skin. It was going to be a form of slow torture. She lifted her hands and poured some more oil in her palms and then went back to smoothing her hands lightly across his shoulders.

Breathing deeply and closing her eyes, she increased the pressure of her fingers letting her training guide her. Massaging Daniel was everything she imagined it would be and more. His muscles loosened beneath her fingers.

"I was right." Daniel spoke softly, breaking the trance she'd found herself in. Rochelle opened her eyes and looked down. Daniel had twisted his head to look over his shoulder at her.

"How so?"

"You are the best masseuse." Before she could react, he sat up, swinging his legs over the table. He placed his hands on either side of her face and took possession of her lips. It was a soft, gentle touch. Her body yearned for something more. Something more intense. Something she hadn't ever experienced in the arms of her previous lovers.

She went to put her arms around his neck when a loud Latin tune filled the room. The sound was so foreign she pulled out of his embrace putting space between them. A groan erupted from Daniel.

"Don't move." Daniel kissed her lips quickly and then slipped off the bed, picked up his pants, and extracted the phone. Rochelle thought he would dismiss the call, but instead, Daniel connected it.

"This had better be good, Adam," he growled into the phone, clearly unimpressed by the timing.

She was grateful for the interruption, if the kiss had continued, she had a feeling this room would have seen more action than just a massage.

Watching Daniel, she could see the tension seep back into the shoulders she'd just soothed. He obviously didn't like what Adam was saying to him.

"Yes, I'm working and not taking a holiday. Why are you calling me?"

"Because I know you and Chad are up to something. Why else would you tell him where you're going and not me or Dad."

Rochelle cringed at the sound of Daniel's brother yelling down the phone. She felt awkward standing there, listening in on a personal conversation.

"Don't you blame Chad, Adam. I only told him I was going away. He didn't know where until I got here. Or what I was planning on doing, no one did. I did not conspire with Chad so drop the attitude."

She couldn't hear what Adam said next, but from the tone of Daniel's voice Adam wasn't letting up in his blasting of Daniel.

"You're in charge of the Tea Farm, Adam not Emerald Paradise. That's my responsibility and you have no say in how I do things. Why can't you trust me to know what is for the betterment of the resort. I wouldn't do anything to harm the resort's reputation or the Whitman name."

Rochelle wanted to go over to Daniel and place her arms around him. Give him support. She'd previously surmised his heart and soul was tied up in his resort; now she knew. With every word he spoke, his passion for the resort became clearer and clearer. And he became more dangerous to her. Her need to help him would overtake her sensibility, and she may find herself sharing her ideas with him before she shared them with the board. She couldn't risk another black mark.

Instead of walking to Daniel, she reached behind her to open the door. As far as she was concerned, the massage and tour were over. It was too dangerous to be in such close proximity to him. She should've stayed strong and not had anything else to do with him while he was staying at the resort.

Rochelle escaped through the door while Daniel had his back turned. Even only hearing his side of the conversation, she surmised he wasn't happy with Adam. As she hurried down the hallway, she knew she was running away from him and what his touch made her feel. It may have been be the coward's way, but it was her only choice. Nothing good would come of an involvement with Daniel.

Nothing at all.

Chapter 6

"If you could make sure you take copies of these and then give me back the originals I'd appreciate it." Rochelle handed over the papers to Melanie with one hand and picked up her mobile with the other. Distracted by the pile of papers that had accumulated on her desk during her recent three-day absence from the resort, she didn't even bother to look to see who was calling.

"Rochelle Harris."

"Rochy?"

Rochelle's heart plummeted to her toes. No it couldn't be. She didn't want it to be. White noise filled her ears and her fingers loosened their hold on her phone as it clattered to the table. Why after all this time was her mother calling her?

"Rochelle, are you there?"

Shaking her head to clear the fog enveloping it, she picked up the phone.

"Hello mother." Her voice sounded strong and confident, the total opposite of what she was feeling.

"Oh Rochy, it's so good to hear you. How have you been?"

What the hell? Her mother was acting as if they'd spoken last week not five years ago. After the last time she called to see if Rochelle could lend her some money, Rochelle had told her mother not to bother calling again. "I'm fine. What do you want?"

"I want to see you, Rochy. Talk to you. I need you to know that I'm better now. I haven't gambled in nearly two years."

Rochelle had heard it all before. Although the not gambling for two years part was something new. Usually her mother said she hadn't gambled for a couple of months, six at the most. She didn't believe her then and she didn't believe her now. She had trusted her too many times in the past, and her mother had disappointed her time and time and time again.

"That's nice. Is there a purpose for your call I'm quite busy at the moment." She had to keep her responses short and curt. It was the only way she could protect her heart from wanting to believe her mother.

"Oh please Rochelle, hear me out. I have got my life in order. I've got a job. I'm paying my rent and bills. I've got help for my addiction. I go to my meetings every week. I want to see you."

Rochelle pinched the skin at the bridge of her nose and began counting to five to stop from screaming out in frustration. "I've heard this all before, Mum. Why should I believe you this time?"

She heard her mother sigh down the line. "I know I don't deserve a second chance but I'm hoping that you'll consider it. It's time to heal."

It was more like her fourth or fifth request for forgiveness dating back to those days in the cockroach infested apartments. "You're right you don't." She paused swallowing over the emotions clogging in her throat. The little girl inside of Rochelle was begging her to consider what her mum was saying. That this time it was true and for real. "I want to believe you, Mum. You don't know how much, but all I can remember is the time I was fifteen. The night when you lost so much money to that loser he knocked you out because you couldn't pay up. He decided I could be a nice payment token for him. I had to push my dresser across my door to keep him out. I was so frightened that it wouldn't stop him. I was fifteen, Mum. I should've been going to the movies with my friends, not scared that I was going to get attacked by one of your sleazy, poker playing friends." She took a deep breath, fighting the emotions threatening to break her control. "So you tell me, Mum, do you think you're worth a second chance?"

"I'm sorry, I didn't know. I never wanted you to get hurt. Why didn't you say something?"

"What was the point? You never listened to what I had to say. Anyway it didn't matter, you were gone off chasing the next big win when I got up the next morning. Although how you were able to always amazed me. Guess your addiction was more important than the well-being of your only daughter." She couldn't keep the bitterness out of her tone.

"Rochy," her mother's voice whispered, a wealth of regret in one little word.

Rochelle couldn't do it anymore. "I've got to go, Mum." She disconnected the call before her mother could say anything else.

She pushed her chair away from the desk. The overwhelming need to get away from the four walls closing in around her was the most important thing in her mind. She rushed out the door past Melanie. Her only goal to get outside before the tears building up inside of her fell down her cheeks. With her head down, she hurried through reception and out the front doors. She rounded the corner and stopped, leaning her back against the rough stone of the wall.

The tears she'd been holding back trickled down her cheeks. Why now? She kept asking the question and couldn't come up with a satisfactory answer. Or an answer she wanted to believe. She was about to embark on a major move with her career and her mother decided it was time to come back into her life.

"Rochelle?"

She jumped as Daniel's hand landed on her shoulder. He was the last person she wanted to see while in this emotional state. After their kiss in the massage room, she'd taken some personal leave and escaped down to Brisbane. She'd needed to have some time away to think and get her focus back on her career. She thought she'd succeeded but she'd been wrong. First day back after her trip her mother calls and sets her world into a slow spin of confusion.

She looked at Daniel; the concern in his eyes almost had her caving in and wrapping her arms around him, needing his strength.

"Are you okay, Chelle?" He cupped her cheek and swiped his thumb under her eye catching the tears as they fell. She leaned into his touch, but when his arms came around her, she pulled away. She couldn't let herself rely on Daniel. He would only let her down when he left.

"I've got to go."

Daniel took hold of her arm again, stalling her retreat. "Wait, Chelle, let me help you. You can't go off upset."

"Leave me alone, Daniel."

She shook off his arm and broke out into a run, heading blindly into the resort's grounds, trying to find solace from the memories snapping at her heels.

• • •

Rochelle sat on the park bench in the garden where she'd taken a Tai Chi class just that morning as the sun rose over the trees. It felt like a lifetime ago. She closed her eyes, taking some breaths to calm the turmoil inside her, aiming for the inner peace she'd had only a few hours ago.

It wasn't working.

A twig snapped behind her. She didn't have to turn around to know who was there.

"Why did you follow me? I wanted to be alone."

Her need for privacy right now was a priority—why couldn't he get that?

He sat down next to her. "I wanted to see you, so yes, I followed you. I couldn't let you go off alone. You're upset." Daniel took her hand in his, rubbing his thumb across the top of it. "I don't like to see you upset."

The sadness that had pervaded her soul since her mother's phone call faded a little at his words. He wanted to see her, even though she had deliberately taken a trip away to avoid him.

"Why do you want to see me?" Rochelle turned to look at him and found herself falling into the deep ocean of his eyes. It would be so easy to let him take her away from all of this. But she couldn't.

"Well, I didn't want to see you for this, but I think you might need it," he murmured as he placed his hands on either side of her face, leaned in and placed a soft kiss on her lips. Her breath caught, and with a sigh she opened her mouth to allow him better access. Their lips sipped at each other, but when she wanted to take it deeper, Daniel pulled away.

He didn't say anything but pulled her closer to him and started rubbing his hand over her back. The touch was soothing, and she closed her eyes and let the conversation with her mother wash away. She appreciated that he wasn't saying anything, that he was simply being there for her.

Rochelle had no idea how long they sat there, but she shivered as a cool breeze glossed over her arms.

"We should probably think about going inside," she whispered against Daniel's chest. But she didn't make the move to break the calmness that had enveloped them.

"If that's what you want."

"I'm not sure it is what I want. I do know it's probably the sensible thing to do. Plus I need to finish up some things in my office."

She pushed away from Daniel's hold, but he pulled her back into his embrace. "It's late and everything will still be there in the morning. Come and have a drink with me at the bar."

Rochelle was torn between what she'd always done: put work first and pushed aside any thoughts of a personal relationship. One thing she did know: she didn't want to end this time with

Daniel. He was too tempting, and she was finding it harder and harder to resist. The fact he hadn't pressured her to talk this entire time on the bench still surprised her. He seemed to know she needed time to herself.

"Come on, Chelle, one drink and then you can go and finish your work if you want to."

Chelle. This wasn't the first time he'd called her by the shortened version of her name. She had to admit she quite liked it. It made her feel special. Her mother called her *Rochy* but that was always when her mother wanted something. It wasn't out of affection or love.

"Fine. I'll have one drink and then I need to finish up a few things. I kind of, uh, left things in a bit of a rush."

This time Daniel let her go when she stood. Her hand itched to reach out and take his, to feel his warmth and strength again. She resisted the urge and they walked side by side back to the resort.

At the bar, Rochelle led them to a booth toward the back of the room. It wasn't fully private, but it definitely wasn't out in the open for all to see. They could have a quiet conversation without too much interruption.

"What would you like to drink?" Daniel asked once she had seated herself on the booth's soft leather cushion. It felt blissful on the back of her thighs after sitting on the hard stone bench for so long.

She knew she shouldn't have anything alcoholic if she wanted to complete some of the follow-up sales figures corporate office required. However, she was tired of listening to her head and being sensible. "I'll have a classic mojito, please."

"Coming right up."

As he walked away she couldn't help but admire the snug fit of his pants over his butt. The image of her massaging that muscular back fired into her brain with the accuracy of an arrow hitting a bull's-eye. She clasped her hands and placed them on the table. Was there any point in denying she found him attractive? If she admitted it to herself, then maybe the desire would fade away.

Somehow she didn't think so. For the first time in forever, her mind was not on work, but on a man she'd like to get to know a lot better than she currently did.

"The drinks will be here momentarily."

Rochelle looked up, startled, so lost in her thoughts she hadn't seen Daniel return to the table.

"Sounds good." She picked up one of the coasters he had placed on the table. She swiveled the piece of cardboard with her fingers. Nervous energy had her in its grip.

"Relax, Chelle. We're just having a drink." He leaned forward and once again laid one of his hands over hers to still her fidgeting. "Unless you want to make it dinner?"

"I don't think so."

Daniel leaned back, taking his hands with him. "Well now, that's a shame, I was thinking a nice dinner in my room would be a great way to finish the day."

A quiet dinner for two away from prying eyes was extremely tempting. But if she did accept his dinner invitation, dinner wouldn't be all that they shared. Her ability to resist Daniel alone in his room would be gone. The waiter arrived with their drinks, and she murmured her thanks while trying to ignore his raised eyebrow at her a guest.

She took a long slip, letting the mixture of rum, lime, soda, and mint slide down her throat, giving her the courage she needed. *Snap out of it.* She'd never acted this way with any of her previous dates. Although none of them had made her as nervous as Daniel did with an invitation to go back to his room.

• • •

Daniel took a sip of his beer and grimaced slightly at the bitter aftertaste. He was so used to the unique brews that Chad made, standard brewery beer just didn't cut it anymore.

He really did want to have dinner with her in his room. He wanted the opportunity to have Rochelle all to himself. Even though he knew the staff wouldn't bat an eyelid at them having dinner, they hadn't the first time. It was important to Rochelle not to be seen in an intimate dinner setting, and he would respect her ethics.

He changed tack; if he pushed the dinner invitation she'd probably get up and walk away from him. "It looks like you're feeling better. Do you want to talk about what upset you this afternoon?"

Her raised eyebrow was the only indication his question surprised her just as much as his dinner invitation had.

"It's personal."

"Sometimes things are better shared with another person than kept inside." After all, he had shared a lot of his personal past with his mother with her; she knew things even his brothers didn't know. He could play that guilt card with her—if he were that kind of guy. If she didn't want to say anything, he'd respect her decision, but he would feel disappointed.

When she placed her drink down, there was purpose in her action. She'd come to a decision. He sat forward slightly, anticipating what she was about to say.

"I received a phone call from my mother."

That was the last thing he expected to come out of her mouth.

"And that's a bad thing?"

"Yes."

She didn't say anything else, and he figured that was all he was going to hear about it.

"It's been years since I spoke to her." She gave him a wry grin. "We don't exactly have the same relationship you and your mother had. It's more of a tolerable strangers relationship than a true mother and daughter one."

Daniel didn't know what to say. He'd never experienced anything but unconditional love from his mother and father. He couldn't imagine not talking with his mother. She had provided him with so much guidance and sound advice. He missed that.

"What about your father?"

As her eyes softened and love replaced the sadness shining in them, he was sure she was about to say that she and her father shared a wonderful relationship. "He died when I was fourteen. We had the relationship you and your mother had. He was always there to talk to me and cheer me up. I still miss him after all these years."

"Aww, sweetheart, I'm sorry." He hated that phrase but didn't know what else to say. He knew all about empty platitudes people said when they found out a loved one died. No one knew exactly how another person felt unless they'd been through it themselves.

"Thanks. You of all people know what it feels like to lose someone special."

There wasn't much noise in the bar and Daniel was grateful for that. He knew deep in his bones that what Rochelle needed was to talk, and he was going to be there for her.

He stood and moved around to her side of the booth. He slid in beside her and stretched an arm across the back of the cushioned bench. He knew he was taking a huge risk encroaching on her personal space, but it was one he was willing to take. She stiffened momentarily then relaxed. He'd done the right thing.

"May I ask you a question?" He uttered the words quietly, almost whispering them in her ear.

She nodded.

"How did your father die?"

"He worked himself to death, literally."

"How on earth could someone work themselves to death?" All he could think of was a workplace accident.

As she reached for her drink, he wondered if he'd pushed her too far. He didn't like being pressured to give out personal information when he didn't want to.

"I'm sorry, Chelle, you don't need to answer that. I'm being very intrusive."

She looked over at him and her eyes were dull and filled with pain. He hated himself for putting that look in her eye. "He died driving home from work. He fell asleep at the wheel. He'd had to get a second job to pay for the second mortgage he'd taken out on the house. Mum never saw what she did to him. All she wanted was the money he made."

"She didn't work?"

"No, Dad was a bit old fashioned and wanted Mum to be a housewife and mother. Only she found that stifling and found her own enjoyment, which involved spending all the money Dad made. "

"I always thought when I get married I'd like my wife to stay at home. There's no need for her to work."

He felt Rochelle stiffen beneath his arm. "What if she had a career? Would you expect her to give it up?"

"I don't know, maybe. Anyway it's not a major point for me to consider at present. I don't plan on getting married for quite a few years, anyway.

"I think I should go."

He gathered her in his arms; he wasn't going to let her leave while she was upset. "No, don't go. I'm sorry, honey. I shouldn't have pushed you to talk about your father." He pressed a soft kiss to her hair, inhaling the fresh apple scent of her shampoo. It reminded him of spring days walking through the farm's apple orchards, stealing the occasional ripe fruit when his dad wasn't looking.

Slowly, she relaxed in his hold. They sat there for a few minutes, not saying anything. He enjoyed holding her in his arms. He wanted more. For the first time in months, he wanted someone more than he wanted to increase the resort's business.

He wanted Rochelle.

"Come back to my room. Have dinner with me."

Chapter 7

Rochelle gave herself one last look in the mirror and smoothed down the fabric of her midnight blue, silk, strapless dress. It was the sexiest dress she owned. She knew exactly the message she was giving Daniel by wearing it.

She wanted to go to bed with him.

He was only at the resort for a short time. He was as career orientated as she was. There could be nothing more between them than a casual fling. It was actually the perfect scenario. Why not have a little fun? It had been a long time since a man had made her feel special. Daniel was able to do that with just one look.

She slicked her lipstick over her mouth. He'd listened to her at the bar, and even though he'd asked hard questions, she didn't mind answering them. No one knew what she went through as a kid. She'd been so good at covering it all up, putting on a false front for the neighbors and everyone at school. No one had any idea her life was held together with pins and those pins were constantly coming apart.

Today Daniel's quiet strength had seeped into her, and she had shared a small part of her past with him. Did she have the courage to share a little more with him? Would he judge her based on what she told him about her mother? She didn't think so. But before she made any decision, she would see how the evening progressed.

She picked up her purse and checked that she had her key, lipstick, and condoms. It didn't hurt to be prepared. It was clear he had the same idea on his mind. Otherwise he would've suggested dinner in the restaurant. Or even made arrangements to go into the closest town.

Rochelle turned off the lights and closed her door, giving the knob a twist to confirm the door was locked. Tomorrow was her day off. She didn't have to end the evening early. They had all the time in the world to get to know each other.

The walk to Daniel's room didn't take long. She stood outside his door and hesitated for a moment. She knew the instant she entered, she was accepting the point of no return between her and Daniel. She didn't know what to call what was happening between them. It wasn't a relationship. It could never be that. *Stop it,* she commanded herself. There was no point analyzing things; she was having dinner with Daniel and was pretty sure by the end of the night she would be in his bed and not hers.

Her body tensed at the thought. She'd never gone for one-night stands, but something about Daniel impelled her to throw all her inhibitions to the side and go for it. But nothing would happen if she kept dithering like an old woman.

Pushing away her doubts, she lifted her hand and rapped quickly on the door. No sooner had she put her hand to her side, when the door opened.

There was no going back now.

"Hi."

"Hey yourself." She stood there as Daniel ran his eyes over her body. She could feel her nipples peaking against the satin fabric and was grateful her bra wasn't lace. She didn't know why he affected her so much and so quickly. It should worry her, but, strangely, she found it liberating. When his eyes took on a slumberous look as he took in the short hem line of her dress, she could tell he was as affected by her presence as she was by his.

"Come on in," he said as he stepped back. Rochelle deliberately moved close to him as she walked in, brushing her shoulder against his chest. His sharp intake of breath told her she'd surprised him with her action.

She placed her purse on the coffee table and turned to look at him. He was still standing in the small foyer of his suite.

"I could gush about this room," she started and glanced around the room. "But I don't think there's any need for it."

His chuckle intensified the feeling of joy she felt at her decision. Whatever happened, she wasn't going to regret this night.

As he started walking towards her, she couldn't help but notice the way his steps seemed almost predatory. She straightened her spine, ready for whatever he was about to do.

He stopped in front of her. There were mere millimeters between them. His hand reached out and cupped the back of her neck. He pulled her forward gently. Her breath started coming in short, sharp bursts, anticipation building at what he was about to do.

"I'm really glad you decided to have dinner with me," he whispered the words against her lips. He then captured them before she could answer. As his lips started to gently assault her own, she moaned low and deep in her throat. With just one touch of his lips, her body was on fire. She wrapped her arms around his neck, weaving her fingers through his hair, ensuring that his lips remained fused with her own.

She opened her mouth wider, allowing his tongue to tease hers. The hand he had used to cup her head was now tangled in her hair. She was glad she'd left it down. His other hand had started its own exploration. She shivered against him as his fingers tip-toed down her spine, the action causing her to arch her back so that her breasts were pressed against his chest. She couldn't wait to feel his hands on her flesh. Perhaps she should've worn a top and skirt instead of a dress—his warm hands could be on her skin right now.

In the next instant, she found herself released from Daniel's embrace. She immediately felt bereft and wanted to reach out and pull him back into her own arms.

Could she dare?

"I think we should eat, before dinner gets cold."

His words had the same effect as a splash of cold water. The words stopped Rochelle from following through on her thoughts of continuing the kiss.

She gave herself a mental shake and with trembling hands straightened her dress. "Umm, sure, if that's what you really want."

Thinking she had herself under control, she wasn't prepared for the sensations that flared to life again when he took her hand.

"It's not what I want, but I think it would be for the best if we did. Otherwise things could get really out of hand before we're truly ready."

Rochelle could see the logic in his words, but it still didn't mean that she liked it or wanted the kiss to end. She gave a short shrug and pulled her hand out of his. "Okay."

She walked away from him to the bank of windows. It was dark outside and with the lights on in the hotel room, the view of the rainforest was indiscernible. She could see only herself reflected in the glass. Her lips had a plump just-kissed look. The back of her hair looked like it had been caught up in a windstorm. As she reached to straighten it, Daniel walked up behind her and grasped her hand in his warm one.

As he slowly turned her around, Rochelle couldn't help but wonder what would happen next. He pulled her against his chest, his arms grasping her loosely around the waist. She sighed and laid her head on his chest, enjoying the sensation of being held against his warm, hard body.

As he rubbed his hips against her, she could feel his hard length pressing into her softness. "I want you badly, but I'm not the type of person who jumps a woman the moment she walks into his hotel room, wearing the sexiest dress he's ever seen."

She laughed and some of the disappointment that had shrouded her since he broke their kiss faded. "Well that's good to know."

She told herself to get it together; they had all night and all of tomorrow to explore each other. She couldn't wait to see his face when she told him that.

•••

Daniel watched as Rochelle forked another mouthful of her creamy pasta into her mouth; he never knew watching someone eat could be so sexy. Then again, maybe it was because of the woman sitting in front of him. From the moment he'd opened the door, a certain part of his anatomy had sprung to life, and over the course of the evening it hadn't stood down. He shifted a bit to try and ease the tightness of his pants. He wanted nothing more than to stand up and pull her from the table, take her to his bed, and slowly kiss every inch of the sweet flesh he knew lay beneath the dress.

"Do I have sauce smeared on my cheek or a massive piece of lettuce stuck between my teeth and you're trying to think of a polite way to break it to me?"

"Uh, no." He didn't know what else to say. How would she take it if he told her he'd been thinking about all the ways he was going to taste her? First, starting at her breasts then working his way down her belly. He almost groaned out loud as his cock was yelling at him to do just that. Forget about dinner. Forget about learning more about her. Just damn well take her and make her his.

He pulled himself up at those thoughts. In all his sexual life, he'd never felt this basic need and urge to mark a woman as his own.

Had Adam felt this way when he'd returned from LA and started dating Zoe again? Is this what Chad felt toward Jen?

No.

He refused to let himself think along those lines. He wasn't in the market for a relationship that led to marriage. It wasn't in his life plan. He wasn't planning on getting married until he was at least thirty-five, which was another five years away. He wasn't going to fall into the marriage trap like his brothers. No matter how much he wanted to own and possess Rochelle.

"Daniel, is everything okay?"

He couldn't let her know how much she was affecting him. He had to get a grip on himself and let the thoughts of ravaging her body go to the back of his mind. Later … he would have her later.

"Yeah, just thinking about—"

"Your resort?" she interrupted.

He almost laughed at the ridiculous thought. The resort hadn't been his main focus for the last few hours, but he leapt onto the lifeline she threw him. Maybe if he could get her talking about work, his body might tone down its urges.

"Yeah, the resort is never far from my mind. I'm always trying to think of ways to improve the service and make it the best of the best." It wasn't a lie exactly, but it certainly wasn't the truth about where his thoughts had been ever since he'd met her.

"It's a tough industry, that's for sure," she replied as she placed another morsel of her dinner in her mouth. He didn't think he'd ever be able to look at a plate of pasta again without thinking about Rochelle and how she could take him to the brink of sexual frustration with food.

He gave himself a swift, mental kick to stop thinking of her as a sexual object. She was more than that to him. But he didn't want to talk about hiring woes and marketing campaigns. Would it be insensitive to broach the subject of her parents again? Most likely, but he could see that whatever happened to her in her past had shaped her into the woman who now sat in front of him. He wanted to know everything about her. The good and the bad.

"Let's not talk about work for the evening. Let's just be two friends getting to know one another."

He withstood the scrutiny she gave him. She had her head cocked to the side, as if contemplating whether what he was saying was what he really wanted.

"Sure, I'd love to hear more stories about what you and your brothers got up to. I'm sure there are many adventures, or maybe misadventures, in your past."

Daniel laughed; it was true. The Whitman boys had a lot of fun growing up. All summer, he and his brothers and neighbor Jacob would play together. Of course, his cousin Ashley had always wanted to be included and they let her. He, Adam and Chad were more brothers than cousins to her. Ashley would crag Jacob's sister Colleen into the games, even though Colleen never wanted to be included.

Those had been fun times, until his dad and Joe had had their massive fight and Colleen and Jacob had stopped coming around. As kids they'd never understood their dads' disagreement over which direction to take the farm in, but throughout school there was an unspoken bond between all of them not to hang with each other. Daniel had to admit he kind of missed having Colleen and Jacob around.

"Where'd you go, Daniel? I lost you again."

Man, he was never usually this vague when he was on a date. "I was just thinking about the fun my brothers and I had as kids with our cousin Ashley and the neighboring property's kids, Colleen and Jacob. We got into some real adventures, and of course, fights."

"Will you share one of your adventures with me?"

Where did he start? There were so many stories he could tell.

"Usually it was me, Adam, Chad, and Jacob who started a war of some sort. Adam and I would be on one team and Chad and Jacob on the other. We'd be tearing around the orchards throwing rotten pears at each other." Daniel shook his head and laughed.

"Let me tell you right now, being hit in the head with rotten fruit is no fun. It's stinks and it's sticky and our mom would hose us down before she'd let us inside."

Rochelle laughed. "I'd do the same. Tell me more."

Daniel reached over the table and took her hand in his before bringing it up to place a soft kiss on it. "When Ashley was visiting, which was nearly every day, she'd hear the noise and come running down demanding that we let her join in the fun. If we said no she'd make herself cry and we'd feel bad. Once we said yes, the tears would miraculously disappear and a big smile would break out over her face. No matter how many times we swore we weren't going to be swayed by her tears, the moment we saw that telltale sheen in her eyes, all our good intentions went out the window. I was always the first one to give in—I don't like to see girls upset. Anyway, once she was in on the game, she'd command us, as the princess of the game, to stop throwing fruit and become her knights to fight her battles against the villain, who was always Jacob. I never understood why she always made Jacob the bad guy."

"Did Jacob like that?"

Daniel shrugged. "I don't know. I guess he was a bit like all of us. Didn't like to see Ashley get upset. But Colleen would always tell Ashley she didn't need anyone to rescue her; Ashley could rescue herself. We were always a little afraid of Colleen, especially when she was wielding her field hockey stick. Then we'd run in the opposite direction." Life had been all about fun when he was kid; now it was all about work, work and more work.

When had his life lost the fun?

Rochelle's pulled her hand out of his hold. "Wish I'd had a brother or sister to play with. Playing by yourself got boring pretty quickly."

He couldn't imagine what it must have been like to have no one to have fun with. No one who had your back. No matter how many times he and Adam and Chad fought, he knew that with one call from him they'd drop whatever they were doing and come to his aid.

"Yeah." The word sounded lame to his ears, and he was at a bit of a loss for what to say to her to take the sadness away. It killed him to see the sadness that had seemed to pervade her soul while he talked about his family.

"I know you still see your brothers and Ashley, but do you still see Jacob and Colleen, or have they spread themselves all over the States?"

Suddenly, the small table separating them felt like a whole continent Thoughts about the fun they'd had as kids hit him hard when he realized he'd forgotten that part of himself. The part that had fun and had been spontaneous instead of the planner he'd turned into. Although this trip was the most unplanned thing he'd ever done since he'd left college.

Daniel pushed his chair out and stood. "Have you finished?"

At her nod, he walked around to pull her chair out, then took her by the hand, encouraging her to stand. The warmth from their connected fingers traversed through him, like a river winding through a mountain, steady and strong, never giving up. He never wanted to let go. Going back to Emerald Springs and Emerald Paradise didn't seem so appealing now, and that scared him. For so long his focus had been on making the resort a success—now he wasn't so sure if that was enough. It had to be though. He had plans for the resort and he couldn't let himself be swayed from that focus by getting caught up in the moment of spending time with Rochelle. He was visiting, not staying a lifetime.

If he reminded himself often enough that his visit was temporary, he wouldn't let himself believe there could be more between him and Rochelle other than a short fling.

"Let's continue talking outside on the balcony. It's such a nice night, and I want to make the most of my time in this beautiful place."

Without waiting for her response, he led her to the French doors, opening one and stepping back so that she could precede him. He'd arranged earlier for the staff to set up small lights and citronella on the balcony. The last thing he wanted was to be slapping at mosquitoes all evening.

He joined her on the small cane couch and slung an arm around her shoulders, bringing her closer to him. They sat together quietly for a few moments, soaking up being close to each other and listening to the night sounds of the rainforest.

He could sit for hours holding Rochelle, breathing in her unique scent. He caught the flowery undertones of her perfume as well as the essence of her. He caught some of the silky, soft strands of her hair and started to twirl it around his fingers.

He tightened his hold when she leaned a little closer and laid her head on his shoulders.

"Thank you for inviting me to dinner, Daniel. I'm having a nice time." The husky tone of her voice arrowed straight to his groin, hardening him even more.

He placed a soft kiss on her head. "My pleasure. I'm really glad you agreed. I didn't think you would."

"I probably shouldn't be here."

"Why?"

He felt her sigh and tightened his hold on her. He couldn't deny it, it was going to be hard to get on a plane and leave her. But a future between them wasn't possible. He lived in Emerald Springs and she lived in this gorgeous part of Australia, worlds apart from each other. Could he persuade her to pick up everything she owned and come live in Emerald Springs, with him? Did he even want that?

"Because you'll be leaving soon. But you're hard to resist, and so here I am."

He chuckled at her quiet confession. "Hard to resist, eh?"

"Don't go getting a big head," she responded, jabbing him lightly in the ribs with her elbow.

"Ow."

She laughed and the sound reminded him of the wind chimes his mother had hanging on their front porch for a little while. "Oh you big baby. Would you like me to kiss it better?"

Rochelle had turned her face to him, and in the muted glow of the balcony, he'd never thought she looked more beautiful than she did right at that moment. He leaned down and captured her lips in a soft kiss. He could taste the fruity tones of the wine from dinner still on her tongue. He wanted to deepen the kiss, but he didn't; there would be plenty of time for him to explore her body. Slowly he pulled his lips away from hers and rested his forehead against hers.

"How about some dessert?"

Chapter 8

Rochelle waited for Daniel to return to the balcony. She'd originally thought his offer meant in-the-bedroom type of dessert. She certainly hadn't expected him to get up, go back into the room, and actually bring out food.

"I saw this on the menu and was intrigued by it."

He was carrying a plate with a meringue confection topped with fresh whipped cream, fresh strawberries, blueberries, and blackberries. Her mouth started watering.

"Oh you're going to love it. Pavlova is delicious. It's my favorite dessert, and I have to stop myself from ordering it each night."

"Great. I was hoping you'd say you liked it." He gave her look that suggested he had something wicked in mind, and it involved the sweet concoction in his hands. "I thought we could share."

She couldn't stop the shiver of anticipation traveling through her body, and it wasn't from the thought of eating Pavlova. "Sounds great," she croaked.

He sat down next to her, holding the plate in one hand. "Do you want some more wine before we start?"

"No, I'm good, thanks." She didn't think she needed anything to make her lightheaded; she was halfway there.

His movements were precise as he dipped the spoon into the dessert, scooping up a generous portion of the layers and holding it out to her. She leaned in, and as delicately as she could, closed her lips around the spoon before sliding them off. The smooth cream was the first thing to hit her taste buds, and it was quickly followed by the berries' tartness and then the combination of the meringue's gooiness and the crispiness of the outer shell. She closed her eyes and moaned. It was so delicious, and this was the reason she didn't order it every night. When she swallowed and opened her eyes, they locked on Daniel's.

"Wow," he whispered and stuck the spoon in to give himself a taste of the treat. She reached and closed her fingers over his.

"Let me." She took the spoon from him and held it up for him to taste. Their eyes remained locked on each other. She watched the play of sensations across his face: the slight flaring of his eyes when he tasted the creamy mixture; the slight grimace when he bit into the berries; the look of absolute bliss when he finally swallowed the sweet concoction.

"I can tell why you love this. Words can't describe it."

"I know. Now feed me more," she demanded with a laugh.

With each mouthful they shared over the next few minutes, Rochelle wanted to reach over and kiss Daniel. There was something extremely sensual about watching another person enjoy your favorite dessert.

"Last mouthful," he said mournfully as he held out the spoon toward her.

"You have it."

She wasn't sure what he had planned as he put the plate on the small table to the side. He moved closer to her until his leg was brushing up against hers. The warmth from his body ignited the sensual fire that surrounded them.

"How about we share it?"

With his free hand, he gently cupped the back of her head. He brought his face closer until their lips were almost touching.

Her tongue darted out to lick a drop of cream that was threatening to fall. Daniel groaned, and the next instant the spoon clattered to the ground and he had his arms around her, his lips meshing with hers.

She wasn't going to fight him. This was what she wanted. Had wanted all night since their first kiss when she walked into his suite. She climbed onto Daniel until she was straddling his legs.

She dug her fingers into his hair, deepening the kiss. Her dress had crept up and she reveled in the feeling of his hands tracing lightly up the back of her thighs until he was cupping her ass.

She pulled her lips away, breathless from the heady rush of emotions that had enveloped her.

"I want you, Daniel," she whispered against his lips. Summoning the courage to ask something she'd never voiced before in her life, she took a deep breath. "Make love to me."

His answer to her request was to tighten his hold around her hips. He moved toward the end of the couch and stood. She strengthened her hold around his waist and buried her face in his neck, kissing the flesh just below his ear.

In seconds, she found herself being laid gently on the bed. The fresh fragrance of frangipani teased her senses. She kicked her shoes off before moving down the bed until she rested against the pillows.

Rochelle watched Daniel as he toed off his shoes and pulled his shirt from his trousers. He started unbuttoning his shirt slowly, teasing her with glimpses of a taut, bronzed stomach. She expected him to shrug out of his shirt and was surprised when he didn't. She was about to ask him when he climbed onto the bed and started crawling the short distance toward her.

She shivered in anticipation. His fingers started a slow trail up her legs: starting at the ankles, teasing his way up behind her knees. All the while, his shirttails tickled her flesh where his fingers had been. She'd never thought that fabric could be sensual, but Daniel was showing her just how erotic it could be. Her fingers itched to take off his shirt so she could run her hands over his skin.

She jumped when his lips touched the soft flesh on her inner thigh. She couldn't take any more of the teasing. She wanted his lips on hers again. She reached down and put both her hands on each side of his face and tugged slightly. "Up here."

He chuckled and moved up, until he was on top of her. He braced his hands on either side of her on the soft pillows. His hands sunk into them, bringing his lips close to hers once again. "Anything for you, sweetheart."

He closed the distance and Rochelle was in heaven. She put her hands to his shoulders, gripping the soft fabric of his shirt. She pushed it off his shoulders and down his arms. He lifted first one arm and then the other to enable her to finally release him from his shirt. All the while, they never lost the connection between their lips. She smoothed her hands over his shoulders before running them down the front of his chest. Her fingers teased his nipples. The action caused Daniel to increase the pressure of his lips on hers. He also lowered his hips against hers and she could feel his erection against her belly.

She wanted all of him naked. She wanted to feel him buried deep inside of her. All she wanted was to be cherished, and she had a feeling Daniel would make her feel like she was the most precious person in the world.

Her fingers worked the buckle of his belt, struggling to get it undone. He pulled his lips away from hers and a chill swept through her. She put it down to having lost his body warmth, not the insidious thought that he would eventually leave for good.

She pushed those thoughts away. Tonight she wasn't going to think about the future. She was going to live in the moment.

She watched as Daniel removed his pants and underwear. He was everything and more than what she imagined he would be naked. His shoulders were broad, giving her a sense that if she got into any danger he could protect her. His abdomen had a defined six-pack and only a light smattering of hair, arrowing down to where he was standing proudly.

She licked her lips in anticipation of feeling all of that power possessing her. She reached around to pull her zipper down.

"Don't." The quiet command stilled her hand. She saw Daniel climbing back onto the bed and sidling up beside her to tug at her zipper. "I. Want. The. Pleasure." He punctuated each word with a kiss on her lips, and each time she tried to make the contact last longer than a whisper.

His fingers brushed against her skin as he separated the metal teeth. He was torturing her with his slow speed. She wanted him to tug it down fast so that she could feel his hands roaming over her flesh. Cupping her breasts. She'd never felt so needy for a man's touch. It was like all common sense flew out the window with one kiss. One touch. One whispered word against her skin.

Finally the zipper could go no further, and she gave him a push so that he fell backward against the bedclothes.

"You're too slow." Her words were muffled as she pulled her dress over her head. With quick movements she had her bra undone and was working on getting her panties off when his hands landed on her hips, trapping hers underneath.

"Don't you know, all good things must be appreciated." He walked his fingers from her hips up to her breasts. He cupped them and rolled her nipples between his thumb and forefinger.

Rochelle let herself fall back onto the bed, moaning at the pleasure strumming through her body. He replaced one hand with his mouth, his tongue laving around her distended peak before taking it into his mouth. She arched into his touch. His free hand moved down her belly until it reached the top of her panties, teasing her with light touches across the edge of them. She wanted him to rip them off. She lifted off the bed and ground her hips a little, hoping he'd take the hint.

He did.

In the next instant her panties were gone and his fingers were dipping into her moist heat. She bit into his shoulder as he consented and delved his fingers deeper, teasing her with light thrusts.

"More, Daniel. I want more."

"Wait," he muttered against her chest and pulled his fingers out. He leaned over her and pulled at the top drawer of the bedside table. He rummaged around until she heard the telltale crackle of a foil packet.

At least someone was thinking clearly. She'd been so caught up in the sensations Daniel's touch had generated, she hadn't even considered protection, even though she put it in her purse. The last thing she needed was an unplanned pregnancy.

Within seconds, Daniel had opened the packet, donned protection, and was lying over her again. His hard length was nudging at her entrance.

So what he was waiting for?

"Are you sure?" he asked quietly.

With those words, he owned a piece of her heart. They were pretty much past the point of no return, yet he was still gentleman enough to ask if this was what she wanted.

She reached down between them, taking his length in her hands for the first time. She guided him to her center and lifted her hips.

"More sure than anything else."

She took possession of his lips as he took possession of her body. Once he was buried deep inside, he stilled, allowing her body to adjust to him being inside of her.

Sensations rippled from her core to the tips of her fingers. She rolled her hips once again, encouraging him to move.

His pace was slow and leisurely, eliciting as much awareness between the two of them as possible. As he increased the pace, so did the feelings inside of Rochelle. She gripped his taut butt, pulling him deeper into her. She could feel her orgasm starting slowly, like his touch, and building until ultimately a crescendo washed over her.

Rochelle called out his name as her orgasm took her to places she'd never been. He soon joined her over the edge and moaned out her name against her ear, the sound sending more vibrations through her already sensitive body.

She held on tightly to him, never wanting to let him go.

He lowered his head gently to the pillow next to where her head lay. His breath came in short gasps, matching hers. He slipped his arms under her shoulders and gently rolled until he was on his back and she was resting on his chest. His heartbeat was rapid beneath her ear. She laid a hand over it, stroking softly as if she could slow the pace down.

Contentment crept through her, relaxing her muscles. Her eyes drifted shut and the last thing she heard was a whispered curse from Daniel as the fingers of sleep pulled her down into their warm depths.

• • •

Daniel waited for a few more minutes to ensure that Rochelle was asleep before he moved. He couldn't believe the condom broke. Never since his first sexual encounter at sixteen had he had a contraceptive failure. He pulled himself away from the warmth of Rochelle's body and went to the bathroom to dispose of the protection.

Once he used the facilities, he sluiced some warm water over his face. He looked at himself in the mirror. He hoped that nothing came of the little accident. He hated having to say anything to Rochelle, but it was the right thing to do, and he always did the right thing.

He walked back into the bedroom and saw that Rochelle had sprawled over the bed in his absence. He chuckled softly. When she was awake she was very controlled and buttoned up. In bed, however, all her inhibitions disappeared and she gave herself over to the feelings they'd generated in each other's arms.

He slipped into the bed, and once he maneuvered himself under her spread limbs, he pulled her close. He was surprised when she seemed to fold in on him and snuggle in. He sighed and let his eyes close.

He was still too wired to sleep. He was strangely calm and contented to lie there holding Rochelle. Listening to her breathe. Knowing that he was responsible for her deep sleep. She murmured and he moved his hand to her hair, starting to stroke it, to lull her back into her sleep.

Is this what Adam and Chad felt when they held Zoe and Jen? He could just imagine what they'd say if he phoned them to ask. All he knew was that even with his most serious girlfriends, he'd never wanted to just lie and hold them. Oh he spent the night at their apartments or they slept at his place, but he never wanted to voluntarily cuddle them. Usually he would give them a quick, postcoital kiss and then they would snuggle into his side and he would put a hand on their hip. The total opposite of what he was doing right now. Tonight he wanted to stay awake so he could watch Rochelle.

You're falling for her, a little voice inside his head said, and he chose to ignore it. He wasn't falling for her. He was enjoying a special kind of intimacy with her. His feelings were probably magnified because of the surroundings he found himself in: the peacefulness of the rainforest and the luxuriousness of the resort.

"You're thinking so hard, you woke me."

Her husky tones immediately pooled in his groin and it stirred to life. He closed his eyes as she turned and kissed his chest. "I see there's another part of you that's ready to go," she murmured against his chest.

He knew he should let her know what happened with the condom first. But he was selfish enough to want to feast on her again. This time, he wanted to explore every inch of her. He wanted her to let go again. He wanted her, period.

"Are you sure?" he asked, which was probably a moot question since she was trailing her fingers down his stomach, millimeters away from his penis waiting eagerly for her touch.

He groaned when her hand closed around him. He gripped her hair when she started to stroke his length, her touch sure and confident. He pulled her head up so he could kiss her. The moment their lips touched, fire ignited and all sensible thought was gone from his mind. He did have enough sense to don protection again, this time making sure there was no way anything could go wrong.

He lifted her up and lowered her over him. Seeing her straddling him, riding him was too much to bear. With one hand he massaged her breast and with the other, he found where they were connected. When he touched her she shuddered, and he felt the vibrations. She was a beautiful sight with her head back and eyes closed. He could feel her muscles clenching around him.

In a quick movement, he pinned her under him. With a couple more strokes, he had her over the edge and he joined her there, awash in emotions he had never felt before.

Chapter 9

Rochelle woke wondering why it was so hot and she couldn't move. It only took a few seconds to realize it was because she was wrapped up tightly in Daniel's embrace.

It had been an amazing night. Yet she couldn't help but wonder if she'd made the biggest mistake of her career.

Last night she hadn't cared about sleeping with a guest, but now, in the cold light of day, doubts crowded in and pushed out the wonderful memories she and Daniel had made.

"Now it's you who's thinking too hard."

He nuzzled her neck and she shivered. Her body responded to his slightest touch. As his hand drifted over her belly, she didn't know whether to let him continue or make up some excuse to get up and leave.

"Daniel, I'm not sure—"

"Don't think," he whispered as his fingers slipped between her legs. "Just feel."

He had a point. Nothing could be solved right at that moment; she might as well make the most of their time together. She didn't know his travel plans, but he'd been at the resort for almost a week. He would be heading back to Emerald Springs soon. After he left she'd be alone and have only the memories of this time together to keep her warm.

She gave herself up to the feelings his hand and lips were creating.

The next time Rochelle woke, the room was much brighter and she was alone in bed. She listened to hear if Daniel was in the shower, but it was quiet.

She got up and padded to the bathroom. She looked in the mirror and wished she hadn't. Her hair was like a bird's nest, and she had black marks under her eyes where her mascara had smudged while she slept.

She looked longingly at the shower; she would love to get in there and stand under the warm water. Let it wash over her and wash away the doubts that had started to crowd her mind again. But she would have to get back into the clothes she had on last night. It was a pet peeve of hers to have to get back into the clothes she'd worn previously after she'd washed. So she'd wait until she got back home to have a shower.

A knock on the door snapped her out of her self-imposed pity fest.

"Sweetheart, are you okay?"

He sounded so happy and cheerful. Where had he been? "I'll be right out."

Rochelle looked around the bathroom and spied the complimentary robes hanging on a hook behind the door. She slipped her arms into the sleeves and tied the belt firmly around her waist. She pulled at the neckline to make sure nothing was showing. Which was completely ridiculous considering all that they'd shared just a couple of hours ago.

"Morning, sweetheart," Daniel said as she flung open the bathroom door. His smile was open and seductive, and her stomach started doing somersaults. She placed her hand over it, willing it to stop moving.

"Morning," she managed to mumble. When he leaned in for a kiss, she twisted her head so that he got her cheek instead. She knew that if he touched her lips, she'd be a puddle at his feet.

If he was offended by her action, he didn't say anything. He took her by the elbow, and even through the thick fabric of her robe, his heat curled around her.

"I've got breakfast set up on the balcony. I arranged it while you slept."

Mortification filled her at the thought of one of the staff walking into the suite and seeing her. She was grateful the bedroom was set off from the suite's entrance, but still, she could've been standing in the lounge when room service had arrived.

"I know what you're thinking," he said as he came up and stood behind her.

"Really?" She turned, crossing her arms over her chest as she looked at him. She lifted her chin a notch. "What am I thinking?"

"How embarrassing it would've been if one of the people you work with walked into the room and saw you with me. Am I right?"

She gave what she hoped was an I-don't-care shrug. "What if you are?"

"Well let me say that first, I'm disappointed you would think I would do something like that. I know how important your job is to you. I also knew you would be having second thoughts about what happened between us." He moved closer to her and pulled gently at her arms until they were uncrossed. "I can't take those second thoughts away, although I wish I could. I don't regret a single moment we shared together. It was an incredible night, and I hope it's not a one-off thing."

He sounded so sincere, and part of her really wanted to believe. She sighed and closed the distance between them. She laid her head on his chest and he wrapped his arms around her. "It was wonderful, Daniel. But you're leaving soon. What would be the point in taking this any further than one night?"

Silence met her words and she knew she'd hit a mark with him. They'd had one night. Tomorrow had arrived and they needed to face some truths. She was starting to feel something intense for Daniel. To keep herself safe, she couldn't let this continue. He was from a wealthy family. He wore it like a second skin. And he would expect his wife to give up her career. She wouldn't do that. She loved her job and her career. Plus she'd seen what happened when you were financially dependent on someone else. Sure, her mother had a shocking gambling habit, and her father had fed it by earning money. But he had to earn money so they could live.

After so many years of being in charge of her financial destiny, she couldn't fathom getting involved with a man who didn't want her to have a career because he could "provide" for her comfortably.

"You could always come visit me."

Rochelle pulled away from Daniel. "I'm sorry, I can't just leave my job when the need to see you takes over me. It's ridiculous to even suggest something like that."

She looked at the food spread out on the balcony and her stomach churned into a million knots. She wouldn't be able to put anything into her mouth without it feeling like it was going to come straight out again.

She needed to be alone. She needed time to think. She needed to work out what the hell she was doing.

"I need to go."

She tried to walk past him when Daniel's hand gripping her arm stopped her.

"I'm sorry, Chelle. You're right; it was stupid of me to expect you to come visit me when the mood takes you. I don't even know why I suggested it."

Rochelle was grateful for his apology, but it still didn't change anything. She lived in Australia and he lived in Emerald Springs in the United States. She didn't even know which part of the States Emerald Springs was in.

She placed her hand over his, relishing the warmth while her heart cracked a little at the thought that when she walked out the door it could very well be the last time she'd see Daniel. He could pack his bags and catch the next flight out.

"I won't ever forget last night, Daniel. It was one of the best nights of my life. But it really can't happen again. I need to go and get ready for work."

The thoughts she'd had last night of spending her day off with him were gone now. She had a major proposal to show to the board. It wouldn't do her any good if she let her focus shift from the most important event in her career to an impossible situation.

"I wish you didn't have to go." He pulled her tightly into his arms and for a half a heartbeat she considered staying.

"I have to. And I'm sure you have things you need to do." She walked away before she changed her mind.

Reaching the bedroom, she quickly divested herself of her robe and pulled on her bra and dress. She didn't want to wear the panties she'd had on last night, so she balled them up and tried to stuff them into her purse. Of all the times to take the world's smallest purse, she chose last night to do it. Giving up, she kept them in her hand. She got her shoes on and glanced around the room where the magic had happened. At least she would always have the memory to keep her warm when she got lonely.

Daniel was sitting on the couch reading the paper when she walked into the main living room. He looked so relaxed, for a moment she wanted to take her shoe off and throw it at him. She wanted him to look devastated at the prospect of her walking out and never returning.

At that moment he looked up and there was something in his eyes that killed her anger in an instant. There was no relief or joy. Instead she saw sadness and disappointment. But with a blink of his eyelids it was gone.

"I would do the gentlemanly thing and walk you back to your door. But I don't know where you live. Can I walk you to your car instead?"

"Thank you for the thought, but I'll be fine. I'm doing the walk of shame anyway. Best I do it alone. I ha—"

"Don't say it."

"Don't say what?" She was surprised at his bitter tone.

"Don't say that you had a great time. It wasn't just great, Chelle," he paused and threw the paper aside. Agitation rolled off him waves, like a six-foot swell crashing the beach. She gripped her purse tighter when his hands framed her face. "It was a once in a lifetime night. One I won't ever forget and one I don't want to end. It should be the start not the end," he finished on a whisper.

He didn't give her a chance to respond. He claimed her lips in a fierce, possessive kiss. A kiss that took and took and took. Before she could truly understand what was happening, he pushed her away. "This isn't goodbye, Chelle."

He stalked away into the bedroom, slamming the door as he left. She had to wonder what his next step would be. Whatever it was, she had to shore up her defenses and repel whatever attack he had planned. She had a feeling that even though he did live on the other side of the world, he wasn't going to give up on her. Would she be able to handle Daniel in full throttle mode? More to the point, how could she resist him if he used his lips and not words to tempt her?

Chapter 10

Daniel wiped the sweat off his face with the towel provided by Kulang's gym. Instead of checking out the spa facilities like he should be doing, he'd headed to the gym and completed his normal weight workout before heading to the treadmill. He was punishing himself but he didn't care. He needed to do something, anything to rid himself of the anger he was feeling about the way he'd handled the morning after with Rochelle. He hadn't even told her about the broken condom from their first time together. He had no idea how he was going to handle that situation.

He'd heard her leave the suite and had wanted to chase after her. But he knew that was the last thing she wanted. He didn't want to embarrass her in her workplace. Now he could understand why she had her own self-imposed rule about not getting involved with guests. He hadn't implemented a hard and fast rule at his resort either about employees dating guests, but because his resort was so transient, it hadn't been an issue. And therein lay the problem with him and Rochelle. He was the transient person. He would be here for another week at the most.

If he were being honest with himself, he hadn't done half the research he'd intended to do. The moment he'd met Rochelle, his focus had been on getting to know her. If Adam or Chad could see him, they'd wonder what happened to their practical, focused brother. He was the one who always had business on his mind.

Business, at least, was the safer activity to embrace. He'd seen how heartbroken his father had been when his mother died. Hell, he had been just as lost. His mother had been so important to him that Daniel wanted her blessing, as stupid as it sounded, when he met his future wife. Deep inside he knew she'd approve of Rochelle.

But no matter what he wanted, nothing would bring his mother back. And he preferred to avoid emotional situations where the loss would upend his world. Again.

His phone buzzed and he picked it up from the console on the treadmill. He swiped to answer without looking at the caller ID.

"Daniel Whitman."

"Daniel, it's Dad. How are you?"

He walked toward the exit of the gym, not wanting anyone to overhear the conversation. "Great, Dad. How are you?"

He didn't ask about Patty. He didn't want to know.

"I'm good. How's the trip going? When are you coming back?"

"Trip's good. They run a really tight ship here. The atmosphere is amazing and the rainforest … well, that's stunning."

"Was your goal a vacation more than a fact-finding trip?"

There was something in his father's tone that made Daniel feel like he was ten again and in trouble for pushing Chad down the grassy hill on the homemade surfboard his brother had made. No matter how many times he told his father that it had been Chad's idea, Daniel had gotten into trouble because he was the older brother.

But he wasn't ten anymore and he hadn't done anything wrong. Well, not really, but his Dad wasn't there and he didn't know.

"How can I know what to bring to Emerald Paradise if I don't experience it? I've already gotten some ideas on how we can increase bookings for spa treatments when guests make the reservations. Not to mention they have a reservation smartphone app I'd like to clone as well."

"But is there anything so unique that will make the resort stand out from the rest? That was the main thrust of your presentation— to bring something no one else has."

Daniel sighed. The fact that his father called gave him hope that perhaps when he returned to Emerald Springs, he could convince them to move ahead with the resort's expansion as well as Chad's microbrewery. But his father was right. He still didn't have anything exclusive to offer at Emerald Paradise. Sure, people would appreciate a totally eco friendly environment. But it wasn't anything new.

So he didn't want to talk about what he hadn't achieved yet.

"I'm still checking things out, Dad. I've got a good feeling that eventually something will show up."

"Well you can't stay there forever."

Stay in Australia forever. The thought had never crossed his mind, but when he'd held Rochelle in his arms last night, part of him wanted to stay with her and forget about everything that had once been so important to him. But at the end of the day his heart truly was married to the resort and Emerald Springs. He couldn't imagine not visiting his mom's grave to talk to her or not seeing Chad's vision of the microbrewery come to life or knowing that, if need be, he could call on his brothers whenever he wanted to. He would miss them if he was on the other side of the world. He would miss not being able to share a beer and a talk with his father. Staying in Australia was simply not an option.

"No, Dad, I'm not going to stay here forever. I'll probably be here for another week, max. I've got treatments booked in the next couple of days. Like us, they use tea in some of them, but I'm sure we can mix it up a bit from what we currently use. Bring in something fresh and different."

"Okay, sounds like you do have things under control. I'll leave you to it, and as it's late I probably should think about getting some sleep. Otherwise Patty will get angry at me for working too hard when I'm supposed to be retiring soon."

Daniel tightened his grip on the phone at the mention of Patty. He had to let go of the anger he felt at the thought of his father moving on. Patty had been their housekeeper for years. He'd loved her like a favorite aunt. But the thought that she could possibly become his step-mother left an acidic taste in his mouth. He didn't need another mother. He'd had the best a person could possibly want.

"That's nice." Even to his own ears he could hear the insincerity in his words.

"Is something wrong, son?"

"Nothing, Dad." He felt like a heel. His dad deserved to be happy. "Really. It's my problem, I need to deal with it myself."

God, he wished they were having this conversation face to face. It would be so much easier to read the emotions on his father's face.

"Daniel, I know how close you and your mother were. From the moment you were born she cherished you. She cherished all you boys, but the two of you … well, I know she knew way more about your dreams than I did. She would just look at me and say, 'Richard, leave the boy alone. I've got it under control.'"

As his father chuckled, Daniel couldn't help but join in. He could so hear his mother saying that.

"I just miss her so much, Dad."

"I know, son. I know you do. I miss her, too. But there was one thing your mother wanted and that was for us to live our lives to the fullest. It wasn't an accident that you were with her at the end. I'd said my goodbyes, but I knew you needed to say yours. I left you alone with her that day so you could have the special time together."

Daniel looked up at the cerulean blue sky, willing the tears filling his eyes not to drop. He'd always assumed his dad had regretted not being in the room when his mom had passed.

He could almost hear her telling him to let his father live his life. And for Daniel to live his life, too. To live in the moment and not plan everything to the *nth* degree. Plans fell through. Life didn't come with guarantees, and you had to live it without regrets.

"I'm sorry. I've been such an idiot about you and Patty, Dad. It's unfair of me. Patty is a wonderful woman; she's lucky to have you."

"I'm lucky to have her, son, and thank you." A soft whistle from Richard floated down the line. "This wasn't what I expected to happen when I phoned you, Dan. But I'm glad we had this talk."

"Me, too, Dad. Me, too. I've got to go and get ready for my sessions in the spa. Count on me to come back with some great ideas for Emerald Paradise."

"I've no doubt. Let's revisit the business plan you presented. I didn't get to where I am today by playing it safe. With the new microbrewery starting up, it probably is a good idea to update the resort. Kill two birds with one stone, so to speak."

"Definitely, Dad, thanks. You won't be disappointed."

"I know that. You won't do anything to jeopardize the company. And if I'm going to leave the three of you with the majority of the shares when I fully retire, you'll all have to work together. I'm proud of each of you, and I know Emerald Tea Farm is in safe hands."

Daniel felt a thrill at the thought that he was going to be able to get the resort into the shape he wanted. Also knowing that he and Adam and Chad were going to take the reins of the company one day filled him with excitement.

He fist pumped the air. He knew if he was with Chad they'd chest bump each other. He couldn't believe that in a few short months, he'd have the resort renovated and ready for the high-class guests he wanted to frequent Emerald Paradise. His vision was really coming true, and it was only the start of him, Adam and Chad working together. Nothing could stop them. The Whitman Boys were going to take on the world. They could franchise the microbrewery. He had no doubt Chad and Jen's brews would become the talk of Emerald Springs and then Washington State and then the rest of Northern America. The possibilities were endless. He couldn't wait to get started. He knew, without a shadow of a doubt, their father would be right behind them cheering them on, even encouraging them.

But that left his uncle out in the cold, and Daniel definitely needed to fix that.

"What about Uncle Sam? Won't he be expecting to have some say in the succession plan? What about Ashley?"

"Leave Sam to me. My brother can do a pretty decent job on marketing, and he's helped you out at the resort recently. But for the overall running of the business side of things, he doesn't have the experience. Sam will understand. Now Ashley, she's a different story. She's market savvy. She instinctively knows what will work and what won't. She's done nothing but positive things for the company. You boys would be mad to let her go."

"You get no argument from me, Dad. I love what Ashley's done at the tea farm."

"You should get her to help you out more with the marketing plans for the resort. She has a flair for style and what appeals to the general public."

Sorry, Dad. I've already found someone who would be perfect to work side by side with me in marketing, and she appeals to more than just the public. "I could, but somehow I don't think Adam would appreciate it. Besides, if I could, I'd lure Rochelle away and bring her to Emerald Springs. She'd have us on the map so fast we wouldn't know what hit us."

"Rochelle?"

"She's the marketing manager here. She has some of the most amazing, innovative ideas; they've really helped put Kulang on the tip of everyone's tongues. She's remarkable, Dad."

"Sounds like you've spent a bit of time with her. Is there something I should know?"

"No, Dad. She's really good at her job." Daniel laughed, hoping it would convince his dad that there was nothing more than a business relationship between him and Rochelle. At this stage, Daniel didn't even know if they still had a business relationship. "I don't think I could convince her anyway. She's pretty committed to the resort."

"Everyone can be lured if the motive is strong. Look at Chad and Jen. Sure, she'd lost her job, but I think Chad wasn't going to stop until he got Jen to work with him."

"That's because he was in love with her. You know he never gives up until he gets what he wants. How else did we get into so many scrapes as kids? It was all Chad's doing."

"Well, I think you've got plenty of charms, Dan. I have a feeling she's something special to you. You just don't realize it yet." He heard his father yawn and remembered the time difference between their worlds.

"Look, Dad, I'd better let you go." He paused and took a deep breath. "Thanks for calling. I've missed having these chats with you."

"I'm glad I called, too. See you soon, son. I love you."

"Same here, Dad."

As he disconnected the call, Daniel felt lighter than he had in months. He was ready to go after what he wanted, and he wanted Rochelle both in his business and his life. He just had to convince her that he was a risk she needed to take.

•••

Rochelle sat on the small back balcony of her apartment and gazed out over the luscious foliage of the rainforest. Every time she looked at it, she was amazed that an entire eco system lived within the confines of the forest. Luckily, the government had recognized its value and didn't allow mining of any sort, even though it was rich with minerals that would bring continual cash flow to the country's economy. She only hoped that no one decided to become greedy and spoil the beauty and balance. She sighed and returned her attention to the papers spread out in front of her. She needed to keep her mind off Daniel and the night they'd shared. She'd felt content and fulfilled. Something she hadn't felt in a long time, if ever. It was dangerous ground. Giving someone that much power over her would only set her up for a fall. Plus, he worked in the same industry as she did. Surely she'd learned her lesson from the last time she got involved with someone who worked at a rival resort. He'd only been using her for her ideas. Fortunately, she'd found out before he had presented them to his board. The Kulang owners gave her a warning, but thankfully they believed she wouldn't freely give away marketing ideas to a rival resort.

Stop it, a voice yelled inside of her. *Stop thinking about him. You're better off without Daniel Whitman.*

As sensible as that voice was, she wanted to ignore it and follow her desires. She'd never let herself live by her emotions. After everything that had happened during her childhood, she knew giving into her emotions would only lead to heartbreak.

A knock at the door sounded, and she was grateful for the interruption. She hoped it was Melanie bringing her the other papers she needed so she could finalize her presentation to the board. She had such a great feeling about this new gong/vibration therapy. It could only bring more people to the resort, to experience this wonderful combination of meditation and healing. She hoped if the board liked her idea, they'd pay for her to go to Western Australia to experience a session. She got up and walked through her living room to the front door. She gave herself a cursory glance, although that was silly. It wasn't as if Daniel had any idea she lived on the resort.

She opened the door and her heart stopped. Daniel stood there looking sexier than he had last night. He appeared lighter in spirit, which only added to his appeal. How was she going to resist him now?

"Daniel, what are you doing here?" More to the point, how did he know where to find her? How did he know this was where she lived?

He held up some papers in his hand and she had her answer—Melanie. "I went to see you in your office, but apparently you have the day off." He raised his eyebrow in query, clearly wondering why she hadn't bothered to mention it to him the previous evening.

Rochelle felt the heat start at her chin and finish at her hairline. "I didn't think it was important." She tried to act nonchalant, but she felt like a schoolgirl caught in a compromising position with another student.

"Uh-huh," he muttered as he thrust the papers toward her. "Melanie said you needed these?"

She was going to have to have a word with her assistant. Daniel could've read this sensitive information listed on the papers and decided to use it for himself. If he wanted something unique for his resort, he was currently holding it. She held her hand out, waiting for him to surrender the papers. Instead, he pulled his hand back and held the documents closer to his chest.

"Not so fast. How about you ask me in?"

What she really wanted to do was snatch them from his hands and slam the door in his face. Her resolve to stay away from him was crumbling with every passing second, and she was wearing sweats for goodness sake. The least attractive thing a woman could wear.

"I don't think so. I'm busy."

"But you can't get anything else done until you get these papers, right?"

How did he know that? She wanted to scream in frustration at his playful stubbornness. Something had changed in the few short hours since she saw him last. "Please, Daniel, can you just hand over the papers so I can finish up what I need to do?"

She stepped back in shock when Daniel took a step into her sitting room. He kept moving forward and she kept retreating. Soon the door shut and they were standing in the middle of the room, mere inches separating them.

His body heat radiated to her, embracing her and making her weak at the knees. She reached out to steady herself and her hand landed on his chest. Her finger instinctively curled into the fabric of his shirt.

She would never know whether she or Daniel moved first, but the next instant she was in his arms, the papers crunching between their bodies. The moment his lips touched hers, she acknowledged how much she'd missed this. They'd only been apart for a few hours. It was ridiculous to feel this way. But as he pulled her tighter to him, she gave herself over to his kisses.

Rochelle pulled her lips away from his and traced the contour of his jaw. "We shouldn't be doing this."

"Why not?"

"Because it's wrong."

"How can something that feels so good be wrong?"

She couldn't think anymore. She didn't want to think. She wanted to lose herself in Daniel's arms. Instead of answering him, she captured his lips again and threaded her fingers through his hair, keeping him close to her.

As his hands drifted to cup her bottom, she moaned against his mouth. He was right. It did feel so good; so surely it couldn't be wrong. It didn't matter that he was a guest and was only visiting. It didn't matter that he could've easily taken the papers Melanie had given him and used them for his own resort. All that did matter was the here and now, and right now in his arms was the only place she wanted to be.

Chapter 11

Rochelle woke to a trail of kisses down her spine. She shivered and stretched. A warm hand slid over her stomach, pulling her back flush against Daniel's front. She could really get used to waking up in his arms.

His lips nuzzled her neck while his hand trailed up to gently touch the underside of her breast. His erection nudged against her buttocks.

"You could easily become an addiction if I'm not careful."

His words made her stiffen. The languorous feeling evaporated. She didn't want to be anyone's addiction. She saw firsthand what addiction could do to a person and a relationship, how it would take something wonderful and tarnish it with blackness.

She went to move away from Daniel's warmth, but he tightened his hold, making escape impossible.

"What's wrong, Chelle?"

"Nothing, I um … " She wracked her brain to try to come up with a plausible excuse. "I need to use the toilet."

He released her and she scrambled out of bed and raced to the bathroom. She sat on the side of the bathtub, trying to get herself under control. She couldn't let him know how his words affected her.

She got up and turned on the shower, hoping that Daniel would respect her privacy and let her shower in peace. As she stepped under the warm spray, she closed her eyes and lifted her face, letting the water cleanse away her thoughts. This was one place they hadn't made love. An image of Daniel standing behind her, his hands cupping her breasts while his lips nuzzled her neck like he'd done just a few minutes ago in bed made her shiver.

Her body started to throb and she could feel moisture building between her thighs. As if she'd projected her thoughts to him, a cold rush of air wafted over her as the shower door opened and Daniel stepped in, reaching out to her and turning her so that she faced him.

She saw the desire darkening his eyes. Giving herself up to the inevitable, she pulled his head down to hers and captured his lips. Everything felt perfect when his lips were touching hers.

After another round of lovemaking that distracted them from finally drying off and dressing, a knock at the door signaled the arrival of the food they'd ordered. She opened the door and took the trolley from the attendant.

"Thanks, Roger."

"Do you need any help setting up your meal?" Roger asked.

Daniel was sitting out on the balcony, so there was no chance Roger would see him if he did come in and sort out the food. Although she had ordered for two, so it was obvious she had someone in her room.

Why does it matter? That ever annoying voice in her mind asked. This time the voice was right. It was her life and she should stop obsessing over what other people thought about her. No one here knew where she'd come from, and they wouldn't judge her because of her mother. Why was she obsessing over it so much?

"No I'm good thanks, Roger. See you around."

"No worries, Rochelle. Enjoy your meal."

As the door closed behind Roger, she wheeled the cart into the room. The smells emanating from the covered dishes had her stomach grumbling in appreciation.

"Dinner's here, Daniel," she called out.

As he walked into the room, her breath caught. He was wearing his jeans unbuttoned and without a shirt. He looked good enough to eat himself. Her fingers itched to massage his broad chest and wide shoulders again, continuing on from the short massage she'd given in at the spa. What would he say if she suggested it? Somehow she didn't think he'd say no. He reached her side as she was lifting the lid off the dishes.

"This looks great. Let's eat out on the balcony."

Rochelle would've preferred to eat at the small table set up in the corner of the sitting room. Out on the balcony, in the muted evening light, it gave their meal a more romantic feel, even though they'd spent the afternoon in bed and she'd just wanted to massage Daniel. For the sake of her feelings, she wasn't ready to keep up the illusion there was more to their relationship than just being bed buddies at present.

"Actually, can we eat inside at the table? I'm feeling a little cold."

He shrugged and carried his plate over to the small dining table. They ate, neither one speaking. It was as if Daniel knew she was feeling a little out of sorts. Losing herself in his arms hadn't solved anything—she still didn't know how this relationship fit into the future she had planned and was working to make happen.

"Do you want to tell me why you freaked out when I talked about you being an addiction?"

The question came out of left field. She thought he'd forgotten all about her reaction to that comment.

"I didn't freak out."

He sighed and reached across the table to grab her hand. "Chelle, I was lying as close as a person can get next to another person. I felt your body tense at the word 'addiction.' Is there something you're not telling me?"

Ah, so he thought she was trying to hide an addiction of her own from him. She looked at their joined hands, his thumb stroking gently over the top of hers. His touch was warm and reassuring. Could she tell him the ugly truth about her mother? She recalled their conversation of just yesterday, after her mother had called. He'd not pressured her to share with him. Was she being fair to him by keeping that part of her history from him? The man sitting before her had opened up to her about his mother when they'd sat by the lake. He'd shared an intimate part of himself.

"I don't have an addiction." She paused and pulled her hand away from his. She clasped her hands on her lap, pressing them together to give herself the strength to go on. "But my mother does. Her addiction is what got my father killed."

Before she could say anything else, Daniel stood. Pushing back his chair, he skirted the small table to where she sat. He pulled out her chair, took her clasped hands in his, and pulled lightly until she stood up. He gave her a quick hug and then slung his arm around her shoulder and led her to a seat on her couch. "I think this conversation would be better if I was holding you. I'm not going to judge you by the actions of your mom. You are a completely different person. And I like the person you are. I like her very much."

"Thank you. That means a lot. I'm not sure where I should start."

"The other night you said your father was killed in a car accident. Just now you said your mom caused his death. I'm a little confused."

It was hard to talk about her past. She had never socialized with the girls at the salon where she'd worked. Nor had she made any friends while she was taking her college courses in the evenings. She was always focused on being independent, having a nest egg of her own that no one could touch, and not needing to rely on anyone for her financial or emotional security.

But with Daniel by her side, his arm around her, she could tell him anything. She knew deep in her heart that even though she hadn't wanted it to happen, she had fallen for him. It was going to be so hard when he left, but she would cope. She'd coped with far worse than a heart broken by love.

"Chelle, honey, it's okay if you don't want to tell me anything."

She wanted to kiss him for being so understanding. She was waffling and daydreaming, something she didn't normally do.

"No, I just get sucked into the memories sometimes." She placed one of her hands on the side of his face. "I've never told anyone about what happened with my mum and dad. Everyone thought it was a tragic car accident. No one realized that he was working two jobs to pay off two mortgages. When we sold the house, everyone thought it was because we couldn't stand the memories. But it was because we had to pay the debts. I gave up school and got a job to make enough to pay for rent and food."

"What was your mom doing?"

"My mum has a gambling problem, or if I'm to believe what she told me yesterday, she *had* a gambling problem. Apparently, she's kicked the habit and has been clean for sometime now. It's not the first time she's said that. Every other time, she's always lapsed back into the habit pretty quickly. I've been burned too often to believe her now."

"I'm sorry, honey."

"Thank you, but there's no need to be sorry. Sometimes we get dealt a lousy hand. I've learned to live with the shitty cards I've been dealt. And yes, I realize the irony of describing my life with a gambling analogy. What can I say—I'm a gambler's daughter."

"I could say my mom got dealt a lousy set of cards, too. You can't be responsible for everyone's actions."

"I know, and I sound like a spoiled brat bemoaning my life when your mum died from cancer."

"No, you sound like someone who has had to fight for everything they've ever gotten. I admire you for that, but Chelle, you can't let the actions of the past dictate the actions in your future. Would it hurt to give your mother another chance? If I could have another chance with my mom, I'd jump at it."

"I don't know if I can, Daniel. I know that sounds shallow considering what you've gone through. On the other hand, if I could get a second chance with my dad I'd jump at it. After he died, my mother took the money that was supposed to keep a roof over our heads and food in our fridge and she bet it on one stupid card game after another."

"Look, Chelle, I'm sorry. It's your relationship, not mine. I haven't walked in your shoes, so I don't know how you feel."

Rochelle fell a little bit harder for Daniel after that comment. He didn't judge her. "Thank you." She leaned in and laid a soft kiss on his lips. They clung to each other for moments before he pulled away. He settled back on the couch and pulled her closer so that her head lay on his chest. His hand stroking her back was comforting, and Rochelle didn't want the night to end. She didn't want Daniel to leave.

"I have something to tell you." Daniel's words stopped her heart. He sounded so serious. She pulled back so she could look at him.

"What?"

"Last night, after we made love the first time, the condom broke."

His revelation was the last thing she'd expected to come out of his mouth. The thought of a broken condom should send fear through her, but her cycle was regular, and she was pretty sure she was safe from any unwanted pregnancy.

Before she had a chance to let Daniel know that she'd be fine, he spoke again.

"I want you to know that if there are any repercussions, I won't shirk my responsibilities. You won't be alone."

His words were so earnest, she had no doubt that if she did happen to be pregnant, he would be there with her every step of the way.

She leaned forward and placed a soft kiss on his lips. "It's the safe time of my cycle. There will be no repercussions."

For a moment she thought she saw regret in Daniel's eyes. As if he wanted there to be a chance that she could've become pregnant. She didn't want to go there. Instead she lay back down on his chest and he went back to drawing lazy circles on her back.

"So I guess I should go," he murmured against her hair, after what felt like a lifetime but was most probably only ten minutes. "Let you get on with finishing the work you were doing before I interrupted."

She'd forgotten all about the presentation. She couldn't even remember where the papers were that he had brought. For the first time ever, she didn't want to work. She wanted to sit on the couch and cuddle. But the presentation was the next step in her move up the career ladder. If she did it right, she'd be assured of a promotion within the parent company of the resort. From there the possibilities were endless. She couldn't let her attraction and growing feelings for Daniel sidetrack her from her end goal.

Reluctantly, she pulled herself away from the safe haven of his arms. "Yes, I've got a lot to do."

"Can I help you?"

Her immediate response was no, but for some reason she didn't blurt it out. Perhaps she could brainstorm with Daniel. She was positive he would not abuse her trust in him. She wasn't even sure there was anyone in the United States actually using gong therapy. She'd only researched the practice in Australia. It would mean their evening didn't have to end.

Deciding it was time to take a leap of faith, she placed her hand on his knee. "Sure, let me clear away our dinner plates and I'll set everything up on the table."

In a matter of minutes the trolley was outside and she had her presentation spread out across the table.

"What are you working on exactly?" Daniel asked.

"I'm looking at bringing a new and innovative relaxation, holistic service to the resort."

"Seems like there's more to it than what you've explained."

Rochelle laughed. "Yes there is; I was just giving you a basic lowdown."

"In the hopes that I might leave it at that and not want to know the ins and outs?"

His eyes gleamed with amusement. She couldn't deny he'd hit the nail right on the head.

"Maybe."

This time he laughed out loud and leaned over the table and kissed her on the end of her nose. "Are you worried I might steal your plans for my own resort?"

Her nose still tingled from his lips. "Well that's what you came here for, isn't it? To find out how we do things so that you can do the same with Emerald Paradise? Would you want your marketing person to share an idea that could put Emerald Paradise to the forefront of the industry with someone from a rival resort?"

"I can't deny what you say is true. My motive in coming here was to see how you carved a niche in the market. I've got some ideas, but I'm not one to blatantly steal other people's work. You can trust me on that, Rochelle. I don't do business that way. And yes, I wouldn't want my staff to share a business proposal with rival resorts. But I can honestly say what you tell me won't go any farther than this room. I respect your loyalty to Kulang; I wouldn't do anything to jeopardize your position here. What I would be open to is a joint venture of some sort. How our resorts could help each other with, say, treatment protocols. And I really like the app you had developed. I'd like to look at doing something similar with my resort."

She liked the idea of working with Emerald Paradise. She'd still be able to keep her independence and have Daniel, too. "It could be a possibility, but I'm not sure how the board will take that suggestion on top of this new treatment I want to introduce."

"Chelle, it's not like my resort is right next door to Kulang; we're on opposite sides of the world. Also, Emerald Paradise is independently owned, just like Kulang. We could quite easily work something out. But I'm not expecting you to do the pitching. I'd do it."

She didn't want to let herself get too carried away with the idea yet. It seemed too big a thing to hope for. Before she could voice any more concerns, Daniel plunged ahead.

"I'm not expecting to do anything this trip, Chelle. We can talk about any joint venture proposal after I've returned to Emerald Springs. I have things I need to sort out there before I can look at convincing my dad and brothers that we should move forward with a joint venture between Emerald Paradise and Kulang. But in the meantime, I'd really like to know what this new treatment is. I'm interested in bringing some holistic treatments to my resort. When Mom was sick, we worked closely with her cancer treatment center to use massage and other techniques to help her fight her disease. I'd like to be able to offer something for their patients."

Her admiration for Daniel grew a little more. His idea to bring something wonderful to cancer patients would definitely honor his mother's memory. But still she hesitated. She could be putting her job on the line talking with Daniel, but she wanted to share her ideas with him. Get his insight. He spoke before she could start explaining things.

"Look at it this way, Chelle. I run a resort; I'm likely to ask the same questions, or close to, the ones the members of your board would ask, giving you an advantage to convince them your idea is perfect for Kulang."

What he said made sense. Taking a deep breath she started. "There's a place in Western Australia that has just been given complementary medicine status."

"What does that mean?"

"It means that they're recognized as providing a service that is effective in dealing with terminally ill patients. They don't distribute medicines, but the technique they use has been successful in slowing the effects of cancer, and in some cases, clear infections that no antibiotic has been able to touch."

"Tell me more. What's the technique?"

" Gong vibration healing."

"As in the gongs they use in Middle Eastern countries? Those big brass ones that are so loud you can't even think? How is that supposed to be relaxing?"

She laughed at the visual Daniel created. Explaining *Resonances'* approach would be a good practice run for when she would meet with the board in a few days. "No, nothing like that. They use small ones and yes, even though it's loud, the vibrations they create go through your body. You see, everything around us is vibrating, we just aren't totally aware of it. But when we get our bodies back in rhythm, then the healing can start."

"Have you experienced this gong therapy?"

"No, I haven't, but I want to. I'm hoping that if the board of directors is keen to pursue this, I'll be able to visit this place in Western Australia and experience it firsthand. I've spoken to the director of the facility, and it sounds absolutely wonderful. Oh Daniel, some of the things she told me are amazing. For instance, after regular sessions of the gong therapy, a lady who suffers from Motor Neuron disease—or I think you call it Lou Gehrig's Disease—has been able to drive herself to the facility instead of getting someone else to do it, something her family never thought she'd be able to again. She still can't talk, but she's been able to get more movement out of her body than she's ever had."

"And you believe her?"

She could understand his skepticism; when she'd first heard about it she'd thought the same thing. "Yes, I do. At first, I was a bit like you, but then I arranged to have a conference call with the client's husband, and he confirmed that his wife had indeed been able to drive herself when before she hadn't." Rochelle paused, needing to take a breath. She got so energized when she was talking about this. "I'm sorry I'm about to sound like a brochure, but there's no other way I can explain this story she told me."

Daniel laughed. "It's fine—sound your brochure best."

"Well, the lady told me they had a little boy who suffers from muscular dystrophy and had a continual infection in his foot. It was so bad that they were going to amputate it, but through gong and other techniques, they were able to save the foot."

"That just blows me away. It doesn't seem real. But what about treating cancer patients?"

"Well, from what the director has told me, the vibration from the gongs help the chemo or radiation treatments go through the bloodstream quicker, which can lessen the after effects of the medication. It can also kill off cancer cells quicker. I've also heard there is an herb that can possibly kill off the cancer cells."

"Again, you believe her?"

"I do, but I still want to meet with her and the people she's treated to see for myself. She told me another wonderful story about a man who was diagnosed with stage four prostate cancer. Doctors told him it was too late to do anything and to get his affairs in order. He went to Resonances and for this herb and gong treatment. That was four years ago, and he's still alive and the cancer has gone."

The more she talked, the more excited Rochelle got. This would be an amazing asset to the resort if they could get a similar facility on site. She had to convince the board to get as excited about it as she was.

"It does sound too good to be true, but I doubt you'd present anything without fully investigating. You're not the sort of person who would jeopardize the resort or even your job. I know you can pull this off, sweetheart. I have complete faith that you will convince the board to back your plans."

Rochelle warmed under Daniel's praise. It was nice to have someone believe in her abilities and believe she could be successful. "Thank you. That means a lot coming from you. Let's hope the words go from your lips to the board's ears."

"Well, if you do get them on board with this project, let me know. We could definitely work a joint venture."

"It does sound like a possibility. Do you have any other ideas about what you want to add to your resort?"

"A few. Perhaps I could pick your brain and you can look over what I've drafted to present to my dad and brothers?"

Once again her chest swelled with emotion. "I'd love to help you."

• • •

Damn, what would it take to convince Rochelle to move to Emerald Springs? They'd spent an hour discussing his initial thoughts on how he wanted to enhance his already existing treatments. Her insights into even better spa improvements were amazing, not to mention he wanted to explore what was developing between them personally. He'd only known her for a little over five days, but it felt like a lifetime. "Are you sure I can't lure you away? Just think Rochelle, you and I together, working on the same team, we could create the most popular and profitable Spa Resort in North America. And that would be the start. We could expand operations here in Australia. Buy up a struggling resort and make it profitable and successful."

Her hesitation was telling. Last time he'd made the suggestion, she said no straightaway. Could she be wavering? Could there be a sliver of hope that she wanted to explore what was developing between them, too?

"It is a tempting offer, but I don't think so. My life is here and your life is there."

Disappointment pooled like a lead balloon in his stomach. He didn't want to leave her. And wouldn't his brothers laugh at him. He'd teased them about falling in love, claiming he wasn't going to get bitten, and here he was looking like he was about to take the tumble, too. Perhaps putting distance between him and Rochelle was a good idea. There was no guarantee that loving someone would last a lifetime. His mother had loved his father, and yet they hadn't had enough time together. His father had recovered and was now moving on, but the thought of losing someone Daniel loved chilled him to the bone.

He pushed the thoughts away. He was *in lust* with Rochelle, not love. Lust would fade away with distance, so until he had to leave, he was going to make the most of his time with her.

He pushed his chair away from the table. "I think we've done enough business for tonight." He walked around to where Rochelle was sitting and took her hand. "I can think of a much better way to spend the rest of our evening."

He smiled when she stood and looped her arms loosely around his neck. She fit perfectly in his embrace. "Really? What did you have in mind?"

He leaned in and whispered exactly what he wanted to do with her.

"I like the way you think."

He scooped her up in his arms, feeling invincible. Nothing could mar what he and Rochelle were about to share.

Nothing at all.

Chapter 12

A buzzing sound penetrated Daniel's slumber. It took him a few seconds to realize where he was and where the sound was originating from: his phone.

"What's that?" Rochelle mumbled the words.

"Go back to sleep, sweetheart, it's just my phone."

"S'okay."

He pulled himself away from her warmth and stumbled toward the sitting area where his phone was. He got there just as it stopped. He was about to go back to join Rochelle in bed when it started ringing again. Clearly, the person was eager to speak to him.

He picked up his phone and his heart leaped into his mouth. It was Adam calling. His brother was well aware of the time difference between Emerald Springs and Australia, so it must be an emergency. He said a quick prayer and hoped his family was okay.

"Hey, Adam, what's up?"

"Bro, sorry to call you in the middle of the night, but it's an emergency."

He gripped his phone tighter. "Is Dad okay?"

"Yes, the family's fine. But I'm sorry, Dan, the resort's not."

Daniel's knees buckled and he gripped the side of the sofa before sinking into the soft depths. All his dreams and hopes were in that resort.

"What's happened?"

"A water pipe burst and flooded the restaurant and function rooms. It's a mess and we need you back here ASAP."

He couldn't say anything. He had bookings for the function room. Hell, Adam's wedding was going to be held at the resort.

He scrubbed a hand down his face, hoping that it would jolt him awake and this would be a bad dream. But it did nothing. He was still sitting on the sofa in Rochelle's room, living a new nightmare.

Something wasn't right.

"It has to be sabotage, Adam. Water pipes just don't burst on their own. There have been too many accidents and incidents in the last couple of months for it to be coincidental or bad luck. Someone is trying to ruin us."

"Calm down, bro. I think you're over-reacting. Pipes bur—"

"God, when are you going to stop being so condescending and start thinking?"

"Look, Dan, check your email. I've got you on the first flight back to Emerald Springs. Once you get back, we can talk about things face to face. I'm not discounting everything you're saying, but it's not something that can be sorted out on the phone."

"Fine, and—" he paused and sighed. "Sorry for flying off the handle at you."

"I totally get it. I know how much the resort means to you. I'll start dealing with the insurance and the cleanup as best as I can. I want my wedding at your resort, okay, man?"

"Okay, I'll see you in a couple of days."

"Shit," Daniel muttered as he threw the phone down on the table and laid his head back against the couch. He wanted to do nothing more than to crawl back into bed with Rochelle and lose himself in her, but he didn't have that luxury. The resort needed him, and he needed to get himself back there as soon as possible.

He leaned forward and picked up his phone again. He pulled up his email messages and opened the one with his flight details.

He scanned the itinerary. Adam had him booked on a flight out of Cairns at 6 a.m. He was at least forty-five minutes away from the major airport. He needed to leave right now if he was going to make his flight.

He glanced over at Rochelle sprawled out on the bed. He couldn't wake her. She had a couple of big days coming up and she needed her rest. He walked over and laid a soft kiss on her cheek. He'd leave her a note on her pillow to let her know that he'd be in touch once he sorted everything out at the resort.

Daniel pulled his clothes on, his mind turning over what he might find when he returned home. He hoped that Adam had exaggerated and it wasn't as bad as it sounded.

He walked over to the table where he and Rochelle had worked on his plans. He gathered up the papers, not paying attention to what he took. Once he had everything collected and in a folder, he found a notepad and scribbled out a note for her.

With his folder under his arm, he walked back in the bedroom and placed the note on the pillow he had vacated.

"I'll be in touch as soon as I can," he whispered. With one last look, memorizing her features, he turned and walked out of the room. As he quietly closed the door to Rochelle's room, he knew he'd left a little piece of himself behind.

• • •

The alarm buzzed and Rochelle reached out to turn it off. She lay still; something was off. She turned her head and saw that she was alone in bed. She reached out a hand and touched the bottom sheet. It was cold to her touch.

Her heart plummeted. Why had Daniel left without telling her? She remembered a buzzing sound and Daniel telling her it was his phone. She flung an arm out and connected with a piece of paper. She picked it up and quickly caught the business card that fluttered out of the folded note. It was Daniel's, with a cell phone number scrawled on the back. She put the card down and concentrated on the note.

Sweetheart,

I'm sorry to leave you in the middle of the night, but I didn't want to wake you, as I know you have an important few days ahead of you. There's been an incident at the resort and I have to fly back to Emerald Springs straightaway. I'll be in touch once everything has been sorted out.

Good luck with your presentation; I know you'll knock it out of the park.
Love Dan xoxo

Rochelle clutched the note to her chest, grateful that he hadn't just loved her and left her. She hoped whatever happened at his resort wasn't too serious and could be solved quickly.

She threw the covers back and placed the note on her bedside table. She was trying not to let the words *love Dan* affect her, but she couldn't help it. Did he mean it? She thought about her feelings for him as she headed to her bathroom to take a shower.

From the moment she'd made eye contact with him, she'd known it wouldn't take much for her to feel something for him. He was charismatic and he had a sexy, smoldering look about him. She had started to let herself dream about possibilities. About letting someone into her life. About letting *him* in. Her past, mother and all, hadn't turned him off. Surely only a man with deep feelings could be that accepting. Or was she getting ahead of herself? Lots of people signed notes with "love," but it didn't mean they were "in love" with the other person.

She could go around in circles and not come up with an answer. Until he said the words to her—if he said the words to her—the sentiment meant nothing. Once he got back to his resort, he might forget all about her. And then what would she do? She had to steel herself against that possibility. Nothing in life was guaranteed. There could be a beautiful woman arriving at the resort right at this minute who could end up being Daniel's soul mate. The thought almost brought her to her knees. She didn't want anyone else to have Daniel—she wanted him for herself.

Rochelle shut the water off on that thought. She couldn't have him. No matter how tempting his job offer was. Her life was not on the other side of the world. Perhaps she should contact her mother and try to rebuild a relationship with her. Perhaps her mother was telling the truth and she hadn't gambled in a long while. Perhaps it was time to put the past behind and move into the future. With Daniel, she'd glimpsed what it could be like to be with someone special, and she found that she wanted that type of future. She wouldn't have to totally give up herself to let another person in her life. Another person who could love her. Pity she wanted the one person she couldn't really have. The one person who had made her feel alive. The one person who was now on a plane heading back to his home.

• • •

Rochelle was at her office when she realized she'd left the plans for her presentation back on her dining table. She groaned out loud and walked back out of her office.

"I've left some papers back in my apartment," she told Melanie. "I'm just going to run back and get them."

"Okay, your first appointment isn't for another hour."

Rochelle nodded in acknowledgement. Where was Daniel at this moment? She knew it was a long flight back to Emerald Springs, and it would be at least another day before there was any chance of him contacting her. If he did indeed contact her. There was no guarantee that he would.

She unlocked her room and walked over to the table where she and Daniel had been working the night before. She stopped when she noticed the clean surface. There was nothing resting on the tabletop. Where had everything gone?

She looked under the table to see if the papers had fallen on the ground. It was clean, too. That's when the realization struck that all her papers were missing, and she dropped aimlessly to the couch, the jolt jarring her tailbone and rattling her reality. There was only one explanation for the disappearance of the papers.

Daniel had taken them.

Now his sudden exit seemed suspicious. She'd spent the evening going over her proposal for something new and exciting, and he'd taken her plans. He had taken everything she had worked hard on and was going to use it for his own benefit to give his resort something that no other resort in the United States had.

How had she been so stupid? How had she let her feelings overshadow her common sense? What was she going to do now? She had nothing she could present to the board. Well, nothing substantial anyway. All her data was in the papers she'd shown Daniel, and she had no time to reassemble the information.

It would be career suicide, but she had to let the board know that she'd let all her plans fall into the hands of a representative from another resort. It didn't matter that the resort was in the States. She'd discussed something confidential, and consequently, she was now in breach of her contract. It didn't help that he was a guest as well, and everyone had seen her showing him around the resort, not to mention having dinner with him.

She only had one choice: resign from her job. She couldn't stay after jeopardizing the chance for the resort to be the first one in Australia to have such an innovative treatment facility onsite. She would tell the board what happened and give them a basic rundown. If they were still interested in the idea, then she was sure they'd get her replacement to liaise with Resonances's director and follow through on the plan. There was no doubt in her mind they'd not beg her to stay, no matter how successful her promotions and ideas had been for the resort. She'd consorted with a rival resort owner and knowingly shared confidential information with him. She'd trusted Daniel when she shouldn't have.

Whether she was making too much out of it didn't matter. From her standpoint, she'd compromised her ethics for a few wonderful moments in the arms of a man who had no intention of ever wanting her for herself, but only for the ideas with which she could provide him.

It was just like the last time she'd discussed plans with a man she thought cared about her. Only that time she had been able to get her plans back. She had no hope of getting her presentation back from Daniel. Not unless she chased him to Emerald Springs, and at this moment, it was the last thing she wanted to do.

Feeling like she had the weight of the world on her shoulders, Rochelle got up, headed out of her room, and back to her office.

She walked past Melanie, ignoring her question, asking if she was okay.

Once she got into her office, she closed the door and made her way to the desk. She pulled up the word program and started to type out her resignation.

With every word she wrote, her heart broke into little pieces. She had no idea where she was going or what she was going to do. She had no idea how she was ever going to recover.

Chapter 13

"How bad is it?" Daniel asked as soon as he got into Chad's Jeep, grateful it was Chad meeting him and not Adam. He'd get the plain, hard facts without suspicion or accusations from his younger brother. After all, Chad had been through a disaster at the family diner just a few weeks ago.

"Well, it looks like it's mainly cosmetic damage. The engineers can't find anything structurally wrong with the building. They don't have any explanation yet on how or why the pipe burst."

"It's sabotage," Daniel muttered.

"Sabotage? How did you get to that conclusion?"

Daniel shifted in his seat so that he was facing Chad. They had a decent drive from the airport to the resort, so he was sure he could convince Chad of the theory he'd come up with on the plane. Nineteen hours stuck in a tin can and a stopover at LAX generally left you with plenty of time to run through numerous scenarios, each worse than the previous one. It also kept his mind off Rochelle. He felt awful about leaving her, but he had no choice.

"Dan, why do you think it's sabotage?" his brother repeated, this time a bit impatiently.

It took him a moment to realize he hadn't told Chad about his theories. Jetlag was a bitch. Hopefully, he'd be able to get through the day without falling asleep on his feet.

"There have just been too many incidents over the last few months. You know we had Immigration turn up saying we'd been reported for having illegals work for us. Then it was the fence being knocked down. A sturdy fence, mind you. Then the unexplained fire at the diner, putting your plans for the microbrewery temporarily on hold, and now my resort. Surely you can't say it hasn't crossed your mind that all these accidents are a little too convenient."

"Well, yeah, it did, but then my mind was occupied trying to get Jen to come back to me and I let the matter drop. Perhaps we should talk to Dad and Adam about it."

"That's going to be fun," Daniel muttered and rested his head against the window. "You still haven't told me what I'm going to find when we get to the resort."

"The function room was under three inches of water. We've ripped the carpet out and have fans and dehumidifiers drying out the subfloor. It doesn't look like there will be any damage to it, which is lucky."

"I suppose, but we only just replaced that carpet six months ago. If the function room was flooded, what about the kitchen and bar—how much damage did they sustain?"

"Enough that it looks like you'll have to replace the appliances in the kitchen."

"Great, there go the expansion plans for the spa."

"I'm sorry, man. Adam is checking out the insurance. I know you have the resort well insured."

"Yeah I do, and hopefully the flood insurance that I pay a fortune for will cover things like this."

Daniel couldn't hold back the yawn and shifted in the seat, trying to get comfortable. He'd spent nearly a whole day sitting down. Now cramped in a car, his muscles were protesting.

"Look, why don't you try and catch some Zs. You're going to need all the energy you have to deal with everything. Plus I want to hear all about your trip and this mystery girl, Rochelle."

"Nothing to tell, bro."

"Uh huh, like I believe that."

His phone beeped and Daniel's heart leapt a little. He hoped the message was from Rochelle. He hadn't left his flight details with her, and now he wished he had. He pulled his phone out and saw that it was a text message from his Uncle Sam. He was tempted not to look at it. But if he didn't, his uncle would keep sending them.

Hi Daniel,

I'm sorry to hear about the pipe at the resort. I'm sure you'll be able to promote your way out of it. After all, you are the master businessman, aren't you?

Uncle Sam

He read the message again, sure he'd misread it. But the words were the same. What the hell was Uncle Sam getting at? He was too tired to think about it.

"Everything okay?"

Daniel sighed at Chad's question. "Yeah, it's fine."

"Message not from who you wanted it to be from?"

"No."

"Bummer."

Daniel didn't want to think about the text message. He didn't want to think about what he was about to see at the resort. He closed his eyes and turned his head, hoping Chad took the hint that he didn't want to talk anymore. A vision of Rochelle as she lay beneath him the last time they'd made love bloomed to life behind his eyelids. She'd looked so beautiful.

He missed her. He wanted her at his side as he inspected the damage. It seemed ridiculous to need someone as desperately as he needed Rochelle right now. The fingers of sleep were pulling at him, and his last thought before he succumbed was of Rochelle and what she was doing.

• • •

Rochelle closed her last case and looked around the space she'd called home for the last few years. The board had been disappointed she'd associated with not only a guest but a rival resort owner. She'd expected that. It had killed her when they'd questioned her loyalty to Kulang, seeing as this was the second time some of her plans had ended up in rival hands. But she was giving her up dream because she was so loyal to the resort—couldn't they see that? She could've gone into the meeting and lied, saying she need a little more time to gather more information, but she hadn't. She couldn't lie to them; it wasn't part of her nature. They hadn't tried to talk her out of resigning or offered to give her another chance.

It had been one of the worst days of her life.

She sat on the bed and contemplated her next move. She had saved a lot of money, so she could find a short-stay apartment complex or buy a ticket and fly to some far-flung place to have a bit of a holiday before trying to find another job. She wasn't sure whether she'd be able to get a decent one at another resort. The board had informed her that they wouldn't give her a reference, and any prospective employer would wonder why, after so many years of service, the resort hadn't given her a recommendation.

The ringing phone made her heart leap into her throat. She glanced at the screen and bit her lip. It was a blocked number. Could it be Daniel calling?

She wouldn't know unless she answered it. Sliding her finger across the screen, she accepted the call.

"Rochelle Harris."

"Hey, Rochy, it's Mum. How are you?"

Rochelle closed her eyes. Her mother was the last person she wanted to talk to. Any other girl in the entire world would have run to her mother at the first sign of trouble. She ran in the other direction. Only she had nowhere to run to now.

"Fine, Mum," she finished on a big sigh.

"You don't sound fine, Rochelle. Do you want to talk about it?"

Rochelle let out an unladylike snort. "It's a bit late for you to step up and play mother, don't you think?"

A sharp intake of breath told Rochelle she'd hurt her mother. She felt a twinge of sympathy. "I deserved that, Rochy. I know I've been a lousy mother. I deserve the contempt and sarcasm you're giving me."

Rochelle pulled the phone away and looked at it. Was the person just agreeing with her, her mother?

"I keep telling you, Rochy, I've changed. I haven't gambled in two years. I go to regular Gamblers Anonymous meetings. I've got a job and I'm now going to buy a house."

Those were the same words her mother had used when she'd called before. However, a new determination had injected itself into her mother's tone. Rochelle had never heard it before. Normally, when her mother had made quick, successive calls, the stories were different and her tone was whiny, almost desperate. Could she trust that her mother was speaking the truth this time?

"I'm glad everything is working out for you, Mum."

Her mother gave a little laugh. "You're still not convinced I'm being truthful, and I don't blame you. Why don't you tell me what's up?"

At the caring note in her mother's voice, the tears she'd held at bay since she'd realized Daniel had stolen her dream rushed into her eyes like a river bursting its bank. "I've really stuffed up and I don't know what to do."

"Oh, baby, I'm sure it's not that bad. You just need to take a step back and look at things. I'm sure tomorrow everything will seem a little brighter."

"I've got no job and no place to live. That's not going to change tomorrow."

"Come and stay with me. I've got a spare room." Her mother paused. "I want to mend our relationship, Rochy. Please stay with me, even if it's only for a couple of days. Maybe there's a job for you here in Darwin. There are plenty of hotels that need an expert marketing guru like you."

Rochelle didn't say anything. She let her mother's suggestion fill her mind. Daniel had urged her to give her mum a second chance. But she pushed thoughts of Daniel aside. It was because of him that she was in this mess.

Or was it really a mess? She had a chance to spend time with her mum. It didn't have to be a permanent arrangement, as her mum said; she could go up for a couple of days, sort everything out, and then leave.

The young teenage girl who'd wanted comfort from her mother when her father died reared her head. Rochelle wanted a hug from her mum, and she finally had the opportunity to get one.

"I'd like that," she whispered past the lump in her throat.

"Oh, Rochy, that's wonderful. How soon can you get here?"

"I'll check out flights and book myself on the first available one."

"Call me back with the details and I'll meet you at the airport."

"Thanks, Mum, I appreciate it."

"You may not believe it, but I love you, Rochy. I'll look forward to getting your call with flights details. See you soon, baby girl."

"Bye, Mum."

Rochelle disconnected and laid her phone on her bed. In the space of an hour, she'd gone from having nowhere to go to starting a tentative rebuild of her relationship with her mother.

Yet she didn't think a mended relationship with her mother was going to cure her broken heart. She had a feeling nothing would.

Chapter 14

Daniel unlocked his apartment and collapsed on the couch. Finally, after nearly two weeks of wrangling with inspectors and insurance adjusters, they'd finally sorted everything out. He now needed to contact construction crews to get the function room fixed in only a matter of weeks so the resort could host Adam's wedding reception.

A knock at the door made him groan. He wanted peace. He wanted to be able to contact Rochelle. He'd heard nothing from her since he'd left and he was worried. He'd given her his business card, which had the resort number on it as well as his email address. He'd also given her his cell phone number so she could get him at any time. Even if she forgot the time difference and called him in the middle of the night, he'd answer her. She'd made her presentation a few days after he left. He was sure she'd call him with the outcome. He had no doubt she would be successful. And maybe that's why she hadn't called. Maybe she was busy planning the expansion.

"Daniel, are you dead? Are we going to have to break the door down?"

He rolled his eyes when he heard Chad's voice. He could deal with his younger brother visiting him. He hoped Chad brought some of his infamous home brew. He could do with a nice, cold beer.

"I'm coming," he called out as he walked to the door. He flung it open and saw his brothers and his dad standing on his doorstep. "Well this is a surprise," he drawled. "How did all three of you manage to get a night away from your other halves?"

His visitors laughed as they pushed past him.

"The girls are discussing wedding plans," Adam said. "We decided we needed a guys night. The thought of talking about flowers, dresses, etc. is doing me in. Besides, we want to explore this theory of yours about the Whitman family being sabotaged."

Daniel looked at his watch and did a quick time calculation. It was morning in Australia, so even if the family stayed until midnight he'd still have a chance to call her.

"Are we keeping you from something, son?"

"No, not really, Dad."

"Oooh, you want to call that girl in Australia, don't you?" Chad teased.

"Shut up, Chad." He was in no mood for his brother's teasing. He was exhausted and really didn't feel up to this little impromptu meeting.

"Boys, no fighting." His father used the tone he'd always used when they were getting out of hand as kids.

"Look, why don't we order pizza?" Adam suggested, always the reasonable guy. "We've got beer, and we can talk and eat."

"Fine," Daniel grumbled. "I hope the beer is cold."

"Always, how can you think otherwise?" Chad scoffed.

Daniel took the offered brew and twisted off the top. He took a few deep gulps and felt a little better. He could hear Adam in the background ordering the pizza, so he went back to sitting on his couch. His father sat next to him.

"I know it's been a tough couple of weeks. You've had so much to deal with and no downtime to combat the jetlag from your flight home. I'm proud of you but I'm worried. Are you sure you're okay, Dan?" Daniel could hear the concern in his father's voice. He really was lucky to have the family he did.

His dad had pretty much summed up how he was feeling and he wasn't up to dealing with Chad's teasing, especially since he hadn't heard from Rochelle and he needed to hear her voice. God, he missed her.

"Yeah, I'm fine. Although, I wouldn't mind reliving the past couple of weeks in a completely different way. But it is what it is. You know me, Dad, I'll be back to myself in a couple of days."

There was no more chance to talk further as Adam joined them in the living room, closely followed by Chad, who was talking quietly on his phone. With the goofy look on his face, Daniel could only assume he was talking to Jen.

"Really, you can't leave your fiancée alone for a half an hour?" Now it was Daniel's turn to tease Chad.

"We happened to be discussing Jen's plans for the microbrewery and her latest brew." He paused and took a sip of his own beer. "Besides, big brother, once *you* get bitten, you'll be the same and I shall take great pleasure in reminding you of this conversation."

"Right on," Adam said on a laugh.

It was hard to stay tired and annoyed around his brothers. They were his best friends, and if he admitted it to himself, he was glad they'd all decided to drop in.

"Whatever," Daniel said. "Now let's talk about all these so-called accidents that have been happening around here over the last few months."

Adam snorted. "I know you want to think there's some sort of conspiracy happening, Dan, but really I think it's just a case of us going through a rough patch."

His earlier annoyance returned at Adam's comment. "Geez, Adam, you can be a real ass sometimes. You're a facts man. Let's look at all the facts. Lay them out on the table."

Adam held up his arms in surrender. "Fine, tell me."

"One," Daniel held up a finger, "after never having any problems with the IRS or immigration, we have them on our doorstep investigating tax and employment records to see if we aren't employing illegal aliens at the tea farm. Two, the fence on the outer paddock gets knocked down and compromises our organic rating, causing setbacks on the expansion plans." Daniel paused and took another sip of his beer. He could see the concern beginning to etch on his father's brow. Obviously as Dan went through the series of unusual events, his father was thinking that perhaps his suspicions had merit. "Three—now this one I'm not sure if it's related or not—Chad told me that Colleen's truck had been tampered with, basically killing the engine."

"Yeah, she was pretty pissed about that, so Alan told me," Chad chimed in.

"Just about everything to do with us pisses Colleen off. She didn't appreciate the bumper sticker encouraging people to drive home to have some of our tea," Adam said with a chuckle. "Although she did agree to that honey deal with you, Chad, so maybe she's mellowing. But I hardly think what happened to her truck is connected to everything else you're mentioning."

"They also had that barn collapse during construction; that could've been really bad," Chad said.

"Well then that is definitely worth highlighting. Next we had the unexplained fire at the diner. It could've been much worse than it was, thank goodness. And finally this water pipe bursting at the resort for no reason. The engineers haven't come out and said anything, but I checked that pipe and to me it looked like someone tampered with it. I think we need to talk to Jacob Sanders and see if he can investigate this for us. What do you think?"

No one spoke for a few minutes after he finished. Daniel was convinced he'd given them enough of a reason to get on board with his idea of contacting Jacob. He may have been Colleen's brother, but Jacob didn't mind the Whitmans, except maybe Ashley. Jacob had teased Ashley since high school.

The ringing of the doorbell shattered the silence that had descended around the room.

"That'll be the pizza," said Chad.

"Either that or you arranged for Jen to come rescue you."

Daniel ducked as Chad threw a cushion at him. "Ha ha. Now give me ten bucks for your share of the pizza."

Daniel reached for his wallet but his Dad placed his hand on Daniel's arm. "Let me buy you boys dinner."

Before any of them could respond, his father stood and walked to the front door.

"We should have Dad over more often if he's going to pay for dinner," quipped Chad.

Daniel laughed. "Somehow I don't think Patty will let him out every night just to pay for your dinner. Besides doesn't Jen cook for you?"

Chad shrugged. "Sometimes."

"You ready for dinner, boys?" Their father walked back into the room with two pizza boxes. Daniel was pretty sure that by the end of the night there would be nothing left.

His dad laid the boxes on the table and they helped themselves to some slices.

"Going back to what you said before dinner arrived. I think there might be some merit in talking to Jacob," his father said after he'd finished eating his slice. "Why don't I contact him? It might be better coming from me instead of one of you boys."

Relief flooded through Daniel. "That sounds great, Dad. It could be nothing, but there have been just too many incidents for my liking."

"Do you want me to come with you, Dad?" Adam asked.

His Dad shook his head. "No, as I said, I think it's best if it comes from me. So now that we've got that behind us, do you want to tell us what you were up to on your trip to Australia? What is this resort like? Do you have any ideas about what you'd like to do with our resort?"

Daniel took a moment to catch up with the lightning fast change of subject. "Umm, okay. The trip was good. The resort is in a class of its own. The rainforest that surrounds it is breathtaking.

And yeah, I got some ideas on what we can do to increase exposure and services of our spa and resort. Let me go get the papers."

He walked into his office and picked up the overnight bag he'd yet to unpack after his trip. He'd dumped the bag in the room and promptly forgot about it so he could deal with the mess at the resort. He carried it back out to the living room.

"So Rochelle developed this app for their resort. Basically when people book they're encouraged to download the app so they can choose which treatments they want."

Daniel placed the bag on the table and unzipped it. He pulled out the wad of paper he'd made his notes on. He flipped through it while a sinking sensation filled his stomach. He kept flipping.

"Oh shit," he muttered.

He not only held his plans but also the research Rochelle was supposed to present to the board two weeks ago.

"Oh shit, I'm so screwed."

"Bro, what's going on?" A hand landed on his shoulder. Daniel looked up and saw Chad standing beside him.

"I've messed up in a major way. I need to call Rochelle now." He looked around at his family. "I don't mean to be rude, but I need to do this in private."

Daniel could see the moment comprehension dawned on Chad. His brother nodded. "Come on, guys, I'm sure the girls have finished their wedding discussion. Let's get out of here and let Dan make his call."

Daniel saw them to the door, offering slices of pizza to go and making plans to get together with them tomorrow. His father paused before leaving. "If you need anything, you call me, okay, son?"

He reached out and hugged his dad. "Thanks, Dad. If I need to, I'll call. And thanks for listening and agreeing with me about the incidents."

He closed the door behind his family and laid his head against the wood. The phone call he was about to make was going to be one of the hardest conversations of his life.

He couldn't believe he'd been so stupid as to scoop up all of Rochelle's hard work. He only hoped Kulang's board didn't hold her accountable for this. If he had to, he'd do a video conference call to smooth things over with them. There was no way he was going to let Rochelle take the blame.

He picked up his cell and quickly punched out the numbers for the resort. He drummed his fingers against the table as he waited for the call to connect. Once he went through the necessary menu items on the answering service, he finally was able to speak to a real person instead of a machine. He would definitely reconsider how calls were handled at Emerald Paradise. "Thank you for calling Kulang Resort. How may I help you?"

"I'd like to speak to Rochelle Harris, please."

"I'm sorry, Miss Harris no longer works at the resort. May I direct your call to her replacement?"

If possible, his stomach sunk further. His worst fear had come to fruition. "Then can I speak to Melanie, please?"

"Certainly, sir, please hold."

Within seconds Melanie answered the phone.

"Hi, Melanie, this is Daniel Whitman. I phoned to speak to Rochelle but was told she no longer works there. Is that true?"

His question was quite ridiculous—the person who initially answered his call had no reason to lie to him.

"That's correct, Mr. Whitman. Would you like me to put you through to Rochelle's replacement?"

Her tone was cold, definitely not the warm, welcoming Melanie he had met at the resort. He sighed and ran his hand through his hair. "No, I want to speak to Rochelle. It's urgent. Did she leave a forwarding number or address?"

"No, she didn't. I'm sorry, Daniel."

"Okay, thanks, Melanie. I'll see you later."

He laid the phone on the table and sank further into the couch.

He was screwed and he'd screwed up Rochelle's life, too. He was so mad at himself. No wonder Rochelle hadn't contacted him; she probably thought he'd gone back on his word and stole her plans. How could he convince her that it was all an accident and that he hadn't meant to take her papers along with his?

He got up and started pacing the room. How could he fix this? He looked again at the table and the scattered papers. Could he send them back to the board at Kulang with an explanation? He snorted out loud; yeah like that would work.

He needed some air. He strode down the hall and into his room and changed into his jogging gear. Maybe a run would help clear his head and help him get a better idea of how to deal with Rochelle and her situation.

He grabbed his house key and IPod, putting the ear buds in and letting the heavy sounds of Bon Jovi surround him. He did a couple of stretches then started running down the sidewalk. While Bon Jovi wailed in his ear about bad medicine, Daniel tried to come up with a reasonable solution to getting in touch with Rochelle. No matter how much he'd like to, he couldn't take another trip to Australia and deliver them back to her. There was too much to do at the resort. Besides he had no idea where she was currently living.

He turned the corner and he caught a blur of movement out of the corner of his eye before he landed with a crunch onto the sidewalk.

The air whooshed out of him, and before he had a chance to take in what happened, a fist landed in the middle of his stomach followed by a quick jab across his left cheek.

Survival instinct kicked in and he thrust out his leg connecting with his attacker. It didn't take him down but his attacker momentarily stopped his assault. Daniel used the opportunity to twist away and stand up. He sucked in a breath, wincing at the sharp jolt of pain in his abdomen.

His attacker had recovered from Daniel's kick and was starting toward him again. His assailant was covered head to toe in black and was wearing a ski mask. When he went to make a move, Daniel was prepared and fended off the punch and landed one of his own.

Unfortunately, he wasn't quick enough to dodge out of the way of a high kick that landed with accuracy against his ribs, followed by another punch across his cheek. He went down on his knees, the wind knocked out of him.

Daniel waited for the inevitable punch that would render him unconscious. When it didn't come he looked up. The man had retreated into the shadows.

"Consider yourself warned." The other man turned and sprinted down the street.

Daniel groaned and collapsed to the ground. What the hell?

He heard a car coming down the street. He staggered to his feet and made his way to the edge of the curb. With one arm wrapped around his stomach, he used his free arm to wave the car down, relieved when it slowed down. He lowered his head, feeling faint, but he couldn't pass out yet.

"Daniel?" A car door opened. "Shit man are you okay?"

"Not quite, Jacob," Daniel said as he passed out.

• • •

"Daniel, can you hear me?" an insistent voice he didn't recognize buzzed in his ear like an annoying fly.

Pain slowly infiltrated his consciousness. He ached all over. "Where am I?"

"You're at the hospital; I'm Dr. Chandler. Can you open your eyes?"

What the hell had he done? He cracked an eye open and saw a woman hovering over him. She had a stern expression on her face. He wouldn't like to get on her bad side. But he hurt so much he didn't care. "My eyes are open; are you happy? Can I close them now?"

"Bro, you always were a terrible patient." Daniel turned, groaning at the stab of pain in his head, and saw Chad smiling at him. Although even in his pain haze Daniel could tell Chad's smile was strained, it didn't have its usual, carefree look.

"Shut up, Chad, you're just as bad."

The doctor, who was poking and prodding him, raised her eyebrows at him and Chad. "Okay boys, don't make me separate you."

Geez the doctor was worse than their mother. "Yes ma'am."

She flashed a light in front of his eyes. "Can you tell me what happened?"

He closed his eyes, not caring if the doctor wanted him to keep them open or not. "I went out for a jog. I turned the corner and some guy jumped me. Next thing I knew, I was on the ground. I got a couple of hits in but it didn't really make a difference. He obviously had martial arts training because he got me with a side kick." Daniel opened his eyes. "I can't believe it happened. I mean it's not the first time I've run at night, Emerald Springs is a safe place."

"Well you're going to be very sore, but you don't have any broken bones. I want to keep you here for a couple more hours to make sure you don't have a concussion." She made some notations on her clipboard and then directed her gaze to Chad. "You can stay for another twenty minutes, but after that you need to leave."

She walked out of the room before either him or Chad could speak.

"I'll hang around, Dan. Until it's okay to take you home. I'll just wait in the waiting room."

"No it's okay; I'll take him home." Another voice entered the room. Daniel turned to see Jacob standing just behind Chad.

"Hey Jacob, thanks for coming to my rescue," Daniel grimaced as he lifted his arm and held out his hand.

Jacob took it in his. "No worries, man, I was glad I came by when I did. Are you up to giving a statement to me?"

Daniel nodded and repeated what he'd told the doctor.

"I don't understand why this happened. What's happening to our town?" said Chad.

"We've had some recent fights at The Rusty Tap," said Jacob. "I'll speak to the owner to see if someone fitting your rough description matched anyone who was there tonight."

Suddenly Daniel remembered the night he walked home from Chad's engagement celebration. "There's something else. Something that happened before I went to Australia."

"What's that?" Jacob asked.

"Well I was walking home and I was followed."

Jacob made another notation. "Sure it wasn't just someone else walking in the same direction as you?"

"No, I don't think so. When I increased my pace, the person following me did, too. Then when my phone rang, I heard them run off."

"Okay it could be related. Anything else you want to tell me?"

Daniel remembered what the person who attacked him said before he ran off. He knew he should share it with Jacob and he was technically withholding information from the police, but until his Dad spoke to Jacob about their suspicions of sabotage, he wasn't going to say anything.

"No, I told you everything I remembered."

"Okay, let me just call the station to make a time for you to come down and sign your statement. I'll be back in a few."

The moment Jacob walked out of the cubicle, Chad walked over to the bed. "Okay, Dan. What didn't you tell him?"

Daniel lowered his voice. "Before he ran off, the guy who jumped me said, 'Consider yourself warned.'"

"Warned? What the hell did he mean by warned?"

"He didn't stick around long enough for me to ask. But I'm thinking my attack wasn't random. Someone is really out to get us. Did you call Dad and Adam?"

"Yeah, I called them the moment I got off the phone from Jacob. I convinced them not come down here. Dad was beside himself with worry. I know it's late but I'll call in on my way home."

"Okay, let him know I'm fine, just a little bruised. Don't mention about what the guy said. I know I should, but it will only make him worry more."

Chad nodded reluctantly. Clearly he wasn't happy with Daniel for not being totally upfront with Jacob or their father.

"Okay gentlemen, my patient needs to rest and you need to leave." The doctor had returned.

"Thanks for coming, Chad. I'll send you a text when I get home."

"You scared me, bro. Don't do it again." Chad leaned over and lightly punched Daniel's shoulder before he turned and walked out.

Daniel ran a hand down his face. This had turned out to be one hell of a night, and he still hadn't come up with a way to solve the problem he'd caused in Rochelle's life. Nothing was going as he'd planned.

• • •

A shiver wracked Rochelle's body and she sneezed again.

"Rochy, I really do think you should go to the doctor. You've been sick for nearly the whole time you've been here."

Rochelle closed her eyes. It hurt to have them open. Her body ached and her mind was fuzzy, like it was filled with cotton wool. "I'm fine, Mum. I'm feeling better today."

It was a lie, but she didn't want to take a trip to the doctors. It would mean she'd have to get up off the couch and walk. Walking required more energy than she currently possessed.

Her mother grumbled under her breath. Rochelle thought she was saying something about her being as stubborn as her father. She couldn't be too sure. Sleep was calling and she welcomed its invitation.

"I need a nap," she slurred before she lost consciousness.

In her dreams, she and Daniel were together again. They were enjoying a wine on her balcony at the resort, holding hands and talking softly. She didn't know what they were saying to each other; all she knew was that it was comforting, and she didn't want that to end.

"Don't leave, Daniel," she muttered.

Other voices intruded on her dream, and with those voices, the image of she and Daniel together faded away.

"I'm sorry, Mrs. Harris, but we're reluctant to treat Rochelle for her fever, at present. Her blood work shows that she's pregnant."

Pregnant? No, that wasn't possible; her mum must have the TV on some medical show. She forced her eyes open.

"Mum?" she croaked out.

"I'm right here, Rochy."

"I'm not pregnant. S'not possible."

"Sshh, baby, tell me, who's Daniel?"

"He's wonderful, so sweet and gentle. He's gone though. Gone home."

"Where's home, Rochelle?"

"Emerald Springs. Tired now. I need sleep." Rochelle slipped back into her dreams. Where Daniel waited again and there was no talk of pregnancy and everything was fine.

Chapter 15

Daniel chugged down another coffee at his desk, his third for the morning and it was only 9 a.m. After he got home from the hospital, sleep had been impossible. The pain relief the doctors had given him had worn off and his body hurt no matter which way he lay. He hadn't wanted to take anymore, but he might have to give in and have some soon.

A knock at the door made him look up. Adam stood in his doorway.

"Can I come in?"

Daniel wasn't surprised to see Adam; he actually expected him to be knocking on his front door first thing this morning. This was his big brother's first visit to Daniel's office at the resort. He had thought he'd drop in before now but Adam was busy re-familiarizing himself with the tea farm operations. The only conversations they'd had since Adam returned from LA had been heated, and at the end, Daniel had always been frustrated. He finally acknowledged he needed an attitude adjustment when it came to Adam. "Sure."

Daniel sat up a little straighter when Adam closed the door. Closing an office door always boded an unpleasant experience. Surely his brother wasn't going to give him a hard time, especially after he was attacked last night.

Adam sat down in the leather chair opposite Daniel, his eyes narrowing as he scrutinized every bruise on his face. Lucky Adam couldn't see the ones forming on his chest. "Are you okay, Dan?"

"I'm as sore as hell, but nothing's broken and I'm here."

"You don't know how glad I am to hear that," Adam paused and shifted in his chair. The action intrigued Daniel as Adam never seemed uncomfortable. "I couldn't sleep last night after

Chad called. I had so many thoughts running through my mind. I really am glad you're okay, bro."

"Me, too, Adam. Me, too." Daniel cleared his throat. Seeing Adam upset at his attack hit something deep inside of him—he'd really missed the closeness he and Adam had once shared. They'd always been a team when they'd been kids, plotting and scheming ways to get Chad and Jacob when the four of them had played together.

Daniel could finally admit it to himself: he resented Adam going away to college and then staying away. He'd felt like his brother had forgotten all about the dreams they shared when they'd been hiding in the apple orchard, imagining how it would be when they ran the family business someday. With their Dad retiring soon, maybe there was still hope they could follow through on those ideas.

"Look, Adam, I want to say sorry about how I've been treating you since you returned to take over the farm. I've been a jerk toward you and, well, I'm sorry."

"Dan, it's cool, man. I know it's been hard on you with me coming back. I know it seems like Dad's ignoring you now. But geez, you should hear Dad talk about all the ways you've improved the resort and how I should speak to you about the tea farm."

Daniel laughed then grimaced as pain shot through his side. "Do you remember all the things we said we were going to do once Dad retired and we were in charge?"

"Yeah, I do, but I think we need to adjust some of our thinking—we had some way out there ideas."

"True." Feeling better about his and Adam's relationship, Daniel switched back to the subject of his attack. "Did Chad tell you what the guy said to me after the attack?"

"Yeah he did. Do you think your attack is related to everything that's going on around us?"

"I do. But until Dad's talked to Jacob, I'd rather we keep that bit of information just among ourselves."

"Dad won't like that." Adam cautioned.

"I know he won't, but after he's talked to Jacob, I'll tell him."

Even though they'd sorted things out, Daniel could tell Adam wasn't happy with his request, but he had his reasons for not telling their Dad yet. The less his Dad had to worry about the better.

"So when we all left last night, it looked like a major disaster had occurred."

Daniel took a moment to pick up on yet another lightning change of subject, but the guilt he felt over how he'd wrecked Rochelle's career prospects returned full force. He still had no idea what he was going to do next.

"Yeah, it's pretty bad."

"Wanna talk about it? Does it involve a girl? 'Cause you know I'm pretty good at destroying a good thing without even realizing what I'm doing. Thankfully, Zoe gave me another chance—a chance I probably didn't deserve."

Years ago, everyone in the family thought Zoe and Adam would get married when Adam finished college. Unfortunately, his brother got sucked into college life, and then a high-powered career and drifted away from Zoe. He was glad Adam pulled his shit together and was marrying Zoe.

"Yeah, there is a girl."

"I take it this is the Rochelle you told us you were meeting with when you were in Australia?"

Daniel shouldn't be surprised that Adam had known exactly which girl he was talking about.

"Yes, she's amazing."

"You know, it's lucky I'm here and not Chad because he'd be teasing you like crazy about getting bitten by the love bug."

Daniel laughed then grimaced as a sharp pain radiated through him, again. Man, he'd have to remember it hurt to laugh. "Today is my lucky day," he noted sardonically.

"So my question is, how do you really feel about her? Do you love her?" Adam quizzed, clearly trying to get to the bottom of the situation.

What did he feel for Rochelle? He wasn't sure. He knew he felt like his world was falling apart. He knew he missed her like crazy. He knew he couldn't live without her.

Maybe he was more sure than he allowed himself to admit.

"Yes," he whispered, surprised that he meant it. He loved Rochelle and he needed to see her. This time, he said it with more confidence. "Yes, I love her."

Adam smiled. "It's an awesome feeling, isn't it? To find the one person who completes you."

There was something so empathic about Adam's words. With Rochelle, Daniel had felt like he could take on anything. He'd even shared with her how he'd felt after his mom had died.

"Yes and I ruined it. I'm not sure if I can fix it."

"Nothing is irreparable. If I can get a second chance, I'm sure you can. What did you do?"

"I accidentally took all her information about a new facility she wanted to introduce to Kulang. It's such an amazing concept, I was thinking that we could do some sort of joint venture between the two resorts. Now she probably thinks I stole the plans so that we could have exclusivity on the facility."

Adam let out a long, low whistle. "Crap, Dan."

"Tell me about it. I tried to call her at the resort to explain but found out she doesn't work there anymore. I can only assume the board let her go. I basically cost her her job."

"It's going to take some major groveling to fix this."

"I know. Only problem is I don't know how to get in contact with her. Her former assistant said Rochelle didn't leave any details, or if she did, Melanie wasn't giving them to me. Basically, I don't know how … " He paused as another knock sounded at the door and his assistant poked her head around the corner.

"I'm sorry to interrupt, but I have a Rita Harris on the phone for you, Daniel. She's quite insistent that she talks to you. In fact, she's getting quite rude."

"Can you take a message? I don't know any Rita Harris."

"I've tried, but she refuses to take no for an answer. She sounds British."

Someone sounding British could also be from Australia.

Harris.

Could this Rita Harris be Rochelle's mother? It seemed unlikely, since Rochelle hadn't wanted to have anything to do with her mother. But what if it was? This was his chance to have a way to get in touch with Rochelle.

"It's okay, put her through."

His assistant nodded and left the room.

"Do you want me to go, bro?"

Daniel shook his head. For some reason, having Adam in the room with him gave him the strength he needed to take this call. "No, it's fine, stay."

His phone buzzed, so he took a deep breath and picked up. "This is Daniel Whitman. How can I help you?"

"By fixing my baby girl's broken heart, that's how."

Daniel gripped the phone a little tighter—it was Rochelle's mother. He was also at a loss for words. How was he going to deal with this?

"Is Rochelle there? Can I speak to her?"

To his horror, Rochelle's mother started to sob. "She's so sick and they won't treat her."

Daniel's heart fell to his feet. He ran his fingers through his hair and wished he was taking the call on his cell so he could walk around. Agitation swarmed through him. He picked up his pen and started tapping it on the table.

"What do you mean she's sick and they won't treat her?"

More sobs. He wouldn't be getting any sensible information out of Rochelle's mother while she was this upset. He tried a different tack.

"Tell me where Rochelle is."

He waited while Rita got herself under some sort of control. "Royal Darwin Hospital."

"Tell Rochelle I'll be there as soon as I can."

"I don't think … "

Daniel hung up the phone. It was rude, but he knew exactly what she was going to say. Rochelle's mom was going to tell him to stay there.

He wasn't going to be kept away or swayed to stay in the United States. The woman he loved was sick and he would be at her side.

• • •

Daniel took a couple of deep breaths as the taxi pulled away. The last time he'd been inside a hospital was while his mother was sick. He hated hospitals, and he hadn't really had time to think about how he would deal with walking into one again. His focus had been solely on getting to Rochelle. He'd rushed straight from the airport to the hotel. He raced through his shower and now he found himself standing out the front of the building that held another woman he loved.

He had no idea what to expect when he got in there. Would Rochelle be awake? Would she even want to see him? Most importantly, would she be okay?

He could do this. It wasn't the same as his mom. He'd known that she had a horrid disease. He didn't know what Rochelle had;

he only hoped it wasn't as serious as her mother had made it out to be.

There was only one way to find out.

He walked into the air-conditioned building, a welcome relief after the humidity of outside. He made his way toward the front desk, the smell of antiseptic bringing back memories of the times he'd picked up his mother after her chemo treatments. She had always put on a brave face, but he'd known she was hurting.

He stopped and closed his eyes. He spoke quietly under his breath. "Mom, if you're listening, or have any sway at all with the big guy, please let Rochelle be okay. Please don't let her be taken from me without my telling her how important she is to me."

Feeling strength wash over him, he approached the desk.

"Good morning, sir. Can I help you?"

"Yes, can you please direct me to Rochelle Harris's room?"

He waited a few moments while the receptionist checked her computer. He clenched his fist against his side, when what he really wanted to do was to drum his fingers on the desk to hurry the girl up.

"She's in ICU, which is located on the fifth floor. She's only allowed family members in the room."

ICU was only for the really sick. He almost swayed at the thought that he might lose her, too.

"Is there … " His voice came out scratchy, so he cleared his throat and tried again. "Is there a room where I can wait?"

"Yes, there is. Once you get to the ICU speak to the nurses at the desk and they can direct you."

"Thank you."

He walked over to the elevators in a daze, trying not to let his mind come up with various scenarios where Rochelle was lost to him. He couldn't lose her, not now he'd finally found the woman he loved and wanted to share the rest of his life with.

Once he reached the floor, he was directed to the waiting room. It was empty when he arrived, and even though his tired body screamed at him to sit down, he knew he couldn't. Instead he walked over to the windows and gazed out. He didn't care how long he had to wait; he would see Rochelle. He needed to touch her. Reassure himself that she was going to be okay.

"Are you Daniel Whitman?"

He whirled around from where he stood looking out the window. In the room with him was a woman he would place in her late fifties. She was still a striking woman. He knew instantly who she was. Her eyes and hair color were exactly the same as her daughter's.

"You must be Rita Harris, Rochelle's mom."

She nodded. Her steps were measured, and he could almost feel the anger coming off her. "You wasted your time coming to see my daughter. I tried to tell you to stay away."

He was expecting this, but he knew he couldn't be an aggressive male with her. He could see the strain in her eyes—the worry she had for her daughter. He met her halfway across the room and directed her to the closest couch. "Nothing is going to keep me from Rochelle. Not if she's so ill that she has to be placed in ICU."

"I think you should go. You hurt my girl badly."

Daniel's guilt intensified. "I know, but you have to believe me when I say it wasn't intentional. I would never hurt Rochelle."

"Well you did. How can I trust you not to hurt my Rochy again?"

"I'm here, aren't I? I came as soon as you called. I'm here because there's no other place I'd rather be." He reached out and lightly touched Rita's hand. "You're not alone anymore. I'm here to help you. Can you tell me what's wrong with her?"

Her shoulders slumped with exhaustion, all the fight and anger leaving her. "She has a really bad case of the flu. Her temperature has been sky high for days. I'm so scared."

Daniel didn't understand what was going on. Whenever his mom had a temperature from her treatments, she would take ibuprofen or paracetamol and lower her temperature in a matter of hours. Surely there was some sort of antibiotic they could give Rochelle as well to fight the infection. "Is Rochelle allergic to some drugs? Is that why they're having trouble treating her?"

"If only it were that simple. She's not allergic, but they don't want to give her anything too strong."

Something wasn't right. There was something Rochelle's mother wasn't telling him.

"What else is going on, Mrs. Harris? I know you're keeping something from me."

She squirmed beneath his look, but then she gave a small nod as if she'd reached a decision. "I was so determined not to let you in to see her. I know what you did, how you broke my girl's heart. How you took her dreams when you left her without so much as a decent goodbye. But a man who would travel halfway across the world to see a sick woman isn't a man who has no feelings. You do care, don't you?"

"More than I ever thought I could possibly care for someone. She means the world to me."

Rita smiled and laid her hand over his. "Do you care enough for her and for her baby?"

Baby?

How was that possible? They'd been so careful.

Except the first night, remember? Yes, the condom broke. How could he have forgotten that? He had pushed away thoughts of a pregnancy after Rochelle had told him she was in her safe part of her cycle. Clearly fate had other plans for their lives.

He was going to be a father? He had no doubt the baby Rochelle was carrying was his. Joy filled his soul. He couldn't wait to see Rochelle's body swell with their baby. His father was going to be over the moon to become a grandfather.

"Yes, a thousand times yes. I love your daughter and I will love our child, too." He pulled Rochelle's mother into a hug. In the absence of Rochelle's father, Daniel knew what he had to do. "Mrs. Harris, do I have your permission to marry your daughter?"

Rita laughed. "Yes and call me Rita."

"Thank you, Rita. Now I can please see Rochelle?"

"Definitely."

• • •

Rochelle's head was pounding like a jackhammer had taken up residence in her brain. She tried to move her head, but it only made the pain worse.

"Hey, Rochy, it's Mum. Keep still—it won't hurt so much."

Rochelle felt something pressed against her lips. She opened them and cool liquid trickled into her mouth. She swallowed around what she was sure were razor blades in her throat.

"No more, sweetie, you can't drink too much."

She nodded but then groaned as the small movement, once again, made her head throb.

"Try to wake up, sweetie. There's someone here to see you."

She tried to lift her eyelids, but they were so heavy. Sleep was clawing at her again. Why was she so sleepy all the time?

Cool lips landed on her forehead and then her lips.

"I'm here, sweetheart; wake up, please. Wake up so I can see your beautiful eyes."

That voice so familiar yet out of place. It couldn't be possible. Daniel couldn't be here. He didn't know where she was. Warmth engulfed her hand and she relaxed as she recognized the touch. Daniel was here in her dreams.

"Come, Chelle, open your eyes."

No, she decided. If she opened her eyes Daniel wouldn't be there. He wouldn't be holding her hand. It was just a hallucination. If she kept her eyes shut, he would stay with her.

"Please, honey, open your eyes just a little. For me?"

"Not real," she mumbled. "So tired."

"I'm real, Chelle, but go to sleep. I'll be here when you wake."

In that place between reality and fantasy, she was somehow conducting a conversation. "Promise."

"I promise."

With Daniel's promise still resounding in her mind, she let herself fall back into slumber, knowing that when she woke, she would find it was all a dream. Just a beautiful dream.

• • •

The next time Rochelle surfaced, her mind was clearer and her head didn't hurt. Her hand felt warm and she figured it was her mother holding it. She kept her eyes shut, trying to grab back the dream where Daniel was with her. She wished with all her heart it was Daniel holding her hand. But there was no way he would be there.

She cracked her eyes open and gazed at the ceiling above her. Boring white. She tentatively started to turn her head, waiting for the inevitable sharp jab of pain. When none materialized, she felt confident in moving it to see who was holding her hand.

Her heart skipped a beat and the monitor beeped loudly. It was Daniel. He was sitting in the chair beside her bed. His head lolled to the side in slumber, but his grip never let up on her hand.

"Daniel?"

His eyes snapped open and a smile broke out over his face. "Chelle, you're awake. How do you feel, sweetheart?"

"Is this real?"

Daniel laughed and rose from his chair. He moved over to the bed and leaned down. "Does this feel real?"

His lips captured hers and warmth flooded through her It wasn't from a fever this time. He broke away from her and she groaned, wanting him back.

"It feels real. Why are you here?" It was then she noticed the bruising and scrapes on his face. "What happened to you?"

"I was jogging at night and someone had a problem with that."

Rochelle knew there was more to the story, but everything that had happened the last time she'd seen him came flooding back. Having to resign from her dream job, visiting her mother, getting sick. "You stole my plans."

She tried to pull her hand away as hurt replaced the joy she had initially felt at seeing Daniel in her room. But he tightened his grip.

"I'm sorry, Chelle. I didn't know I had your plans until a couple of days ago. The resort was a mess and I didn't open my bag straightaway to clear it out. Believe me when I tell you that I didn't deliberately take them. I wouldn't do that to you. I wouldn't do that to us."

"I want to believe you, but I don't know if I can. You left the day after I shared my ideas with you. You took everything."

Daniel sat on the bed next to her and took her face between his hands. She looked into his eyes and could see the sincerity shining in them. "Rochelle, I would never, ever do anything to hurt you. Honey," he paused and placed a soft kiss on her lips. "I've never said this to anyone. I love you, Rochelle."

"Really?" She couldn't think of anything else to say. Her heart was bursting and her ability to speak was gone.

"Yes, really." He punctuated his words with kisses on her lips before placing a hand over her stomach. "I love you and our baby."

"Baby?" she asked. Why on earth would he think she was pregnant? She was about to voice her thoughts out loud when a conversation came back to her. A doctor saying they wouldn't treat her because of the baby. She'd thought it had been another dream. "I'm pregnant? How?"

"Well the usual way is how it happened." Daniel moved back and looked at her, questions mingling with humor in his eyes. "You didn't know you were pregnant?"

She shook her head. She placed her hands over her belly and looked up at him. "I'm really pregnant? We're having a baby?"

"Yes, honey, we are."

"Oh my goodness." Then another thought hit her. She'd been so out of it over the last few days. "Is the baby okay?"

"I'm not sure. We can ask the doctor. They've done everything in their power to make sure they didn't give you anything to harm the baby."

Tears filled her eyes at the thought that something could be wrong. She may only have known about the baby for a few minutes, but it was long enough for her love it. "I'm scared, Daniel."

Daniel gathered her up in his strong arms and placed a soft kiss on her hair. "Everything will be fine, Chelle. After all we've been through, nothing could possibly be wrong with our child."

"I hope you're right."

They sat there for a few minutes before Daniel returned to his chair where he'd laid his jacket. She saw him reach into a pocket and pull out something. He came back to her bedside, picking up her hand.

"Rochelle, my life has been so empty since my mom died. Only I didn't realize it until I met you. You've given me the strength to face my grief and you've opened up my heart to love. An emotion I was too afraid to feel. I'm not doing this because you're pregnant. I didn't know about the baby when I arrived. All I know is when I heard that you were gravely ill, my world just about ended." He placed a diamond ring on the tip of her ring finger on her left hand. "I love you, Rochelle Harris. I love our baby. I want to make a family with you. Will you marry me?"

She wanted to shout out yes but she remembered what he'd said about his wife not working, and even though she knew she loved him, Rochelle didn't think she could give up her career.

"What about my career, Daniel. Do you expect me to give that up to be your wife?"

"No, never." She went to say something but he laid a soft kiss on her lips. "I know what I said, but I also know your career is important to you. Your dedication to your work has made you the person you are today. The person I fell in love with. I couldn't take that away from you. I want you to work beside me, be my partner in every way."

In her heart she believed, but her mind needed a little more convincing. "And what about after the baby is born, would you expect me to be a stay at home mum?"

"Chelle, sweetheart, I want you to do whatever makes you happy. You make whatever decision you want to make and I'll agree with it one hundred percent. I just want you to be happy and I want you to marry me, desperately."

She didn't know what she was going to feel once the baby was born but Daniel's words convinced her that no matter what she decided, he wouldn't be disappointed in her. She loved him with her whole heart, and like him had been half a person since he'd left. In the few minutes he'd been with her, in this room, she'd felt complete. She had her answer. She knew what she was going to do.

"Yes, Daniel, yes. I love you, too. So much, and it killed me when I found that you'd taken my plans."

"I'm so sorry about that. I can't forgive myself for causing you so much distress. I only hope that I can make it up to you."

"You have nothing to make up to me. You came here to be by my side when I was sick, that's an apology enough. I love you, and again, yes, I'll marry you, work beside you, and build a family with you."

He slipped the ring on and it fit perfectly. Rochelle could feel the tears as they trickled down her face. How could she be so lucky as to have the love of this wonderful man?

She reached up and pulled Daniel's head to hers. "You need to seal the proposal," she whispered mere inches from his lips.

"My pleasure." He closed the gap and connected their lips. Nothing had ever felt so right. Together she knew they could take on the world.

Chapter 16

"Are you sure you want to do this?" Rochelle asked Daniel as she smoothed down the fabric of her silky, white dress.

It had been two weeks since Daniel had arrived at the hospital. A scan revealed their baby was growing and showed no signs of being affected by Rochelle's illness. She would still need a few tests but all looked good so far.

"More sure than I am of anything in the world. We can have a party, and if we have to, another ceremony back in Emerald Springs. But I can't wait a moment longer to make you mine. So, Rochelle Harris, are you ready to become Rochelle Whitman and run Emerald Paradise Resort with me?"

She was so excited to be going back to Emerald Springs with Daniel. They'd spent the last two weeks discussing how and what they were going to do to bring his vision for the resort to life. She couldn't wait to get started. They'd even spoken with the board of Kulang and Resonances's director. A joint venture between the three of them was going to see gong/vibration facilities at both resorts. It was an opportunity to make her mark as an innovative marketer and to do it with the man she loved. Nothing could be better.

"Yes, Daniel, yes to everything. To marrying you now. To running the resort with you. To being a mum to your children. I want it all, and I want it with you."

"Then what are we waiting for?" he asked.

"Nothing, let's do it."

Together they walked up the stairs to the courthouse entry where her mother waited for them. Rochelle couldn't believe how close she and her mother had become. After she sorted out a passport and visa, Rita was going to come to Emerald Springs and help Rochelle prepare for the birth. Rita was determined to be a much better grandmother than a mother. Also, there wasn't a casino within driving distance of Emerald Springs. Although Rochelle had no doubt her mother wasn't going to gamble again.

Daniel paused at the top of the stairs and she looked at him quizzically. "What's wrong?"

"Nothing. I just wanted to imprint this image on my mind forever. I love you, Rochelle Harris."

She melted at the love bursting out of him. Nothing could be better than this moment in her life.

"I love you, too. Now let's get married."

About the Author

Nicole Flockton is an Australian living in Houston. She writes contemporary romances and enjoys creating characters and situations unique to them. When she's not writing romance, she is busy looking after her own personal hero, her husband, and two children. Her books include *Masquerade, Rescuing Dawn*, and *Seducing Phoebe*. You can find out more about her at www.nicoleflockton.com, on Facebook at *https://www.facebook.com/NicoleFlockton*, and on Twitter @NicoleFlockton.

A Sneak Peek from Emerald Springs Legacy, Book Five
From *Ashley's Allegiance* by Robyn Neeley

Deputy Sheriff Jacob Sanders didn't know what he did to deserve this, but it could arguably be the best day of his life.

"Uncuff me." Ashley Whitman twisted her hands from behind her back. "This is so not happening." She stood outside the Emerald Springs sheriff's station in a skin-revealing pink tank top and tight, black yoga pants. Her long, wavy, blonde hair curved around her neck in a messy ponytail. "You can't arrest me."

Jacob stood behind her, trying his best to hide the smile that threatened any minute to overtake his entire face. He'd waited for a moment like this since high school. Now that it was here, he wanted to savor every single glorious second.

Ashley blew out a breath. "Are you going to stand back there? Say something."

"Okay, princess." His voice was deep and in control. "This is how it's going to work. I'll escort you inside where we'll be taking your picture. Then one of those French nails of yours will get a little dirty."

"You're fingerprinting me?" She struggled. "This is ridiculous. You can't arrest me. I'm … I'm … I'm a Whitman!"

Jacob threw his head back and let out a hearty laugh. Watching Ashley squirm was priceless. "Don't think your pedigree is going to help you out now."

"Whatever. When do I get my phone call?"

"After I hand you over." Truth be told, he'd already gone ahead and made that call for her while she stewed in the back seat of his squad car. That person should be arriving any second.

As if on cue, Chad Whitman zipped into the parking lot in his Jeep Wrangler. The sides and top had been chucked and an indie rock tune blared from the radio. While Jacob enjoyed riding shotgun along with his buddy every once in a while through the dirt roads of the Skagit Valley, he had busted Chad a time or two for his alternative taste. He was more a country music, boots kickin' kind of guy.

Jacob thought Chad, the youngest of the Whitman boys and his pal since high school, would be the best one to come get Ashley after he was done messing with her. God knows she probably wouldn't allow Jacob to drive her home. He'd hinted to Chad it wasn't anything serious and that he was just teaching her a lesson.

Chad jumped out of his Jeep and greeted them. "I knew this day would come. What'd my beautiful cousin do, deputy?" he asked, his voice deadpan.

"Nothing," Ashley responded through gritted teeth. "I did absolutely nothing to deserve this law enforcement brutality."

Chad looked down at her cuffed hands. "Geez, Ashley, it's only 9 AM."

"Just get me out of these, please." She nodded behind her shoulder.

"Care to fill me in?" Chad asked Jacob.

"It was all a misunderstanding," she answered for him.

Jacob laughed sarcastically. "I wouldn't exactly call assaulting an officer of the law a misunderstanding."

"Oh, please. I barely touched you." She turned to Chad. "Some of the girls, including your bride-to-be, were doing some stretches in the park. We do a little Zumba a few morning before work. That's hardly a crime. I'm certified, for God's sake."

Chad raised a curious eyebrow. "That's where Jen ran off to at the crack of dawn?"

Jacob had forgotten that his buddy was newly engaged. Lucky man. Jen had turned his own head when she first blew into town. He'd never admit that to Chad.

Ashley glared at Jacob. "Some of the girls asked me to help them get in shape for Zoe and Adam's wedding."

"Jen doesn't need it," Chad retorted. "She's perfect just the way she is."

Jacob jumped in. "Um … can we get back to the issue at hand?" He adjusted his deputy hat. It'd been raining in Emerald Springs over the last week, but today the morning sun beat down on his head. "We've had some complaints."

"Complaints?" Chad asked.

Ashley sighed. "So our music was a bit loud. I'll turn it down next time."

Jacob smirked. "I'm not talking about the music." His gaze slid up Ashley's workout attire, resting on her pink top. Actually, more like workout bra. Wrapped around her chest, it didn't leave much to the imagination. Not that Jacob thought of her in that way. It was *Ashley Whitman,* after all. She got under his skin on a good day.

Chad grew impatient. "Then what did they do? Is Jen in trouble? I should call her." He reached in his pocket for his cell phone.

Ashley wiggled her hands behind her back. "Um … earth to Chad. She's not the one in handcuffs. Your innocent cousin could use a little help here!"

Jacob tried his best not to smile at the Christmas present in front of him. Not ready to return it, he grabbed Ashley's arm and led her inside the station. "There have been some complaints about the women showing off too much skin," he explained to Chad, pointing to Ashley's top. "They've been distracting the men's running club."

"Seriously?" Chad raised a more than curious eyebrow. "The men have been complaining?"

Jacob laughed. "More like their wives."

Ashley rolled her eyes. "Oh, please. It's not like we're sleeping with any of their husbands."

Chad came up beside her and yanked her ponytail. "None of you better be. So why did you hit Jacob?"

Ashley shrugged.

"She wouldn't leave, so I grabbed her arm. That's when she went all Fight Club." Jacob karate chopped the air.

"I barely touched you. Trust me, Jacob Sanders, there would be a mark if I hit you hard."

Chad inserted himself between the two, pulling Jacob aside to talk privately. "Okay, you and I know you are not going to arrest her. Can you take the handcuffs off before she totally loses it?'

Jacob smirked at his buddy. Although the feud between the Sanders and the Whitmans ran deep since their fathers dissolved their partnership in WhitSand Farm twenty years ago, Jacob had never held a grudge. His sister, Colleen, on the other hand, would rather starve than eat anything containing ingredients from the Whitman farm. Now that she seemed to be craving everything in sight, perhaps her taste buds would cave in.

He'd grown up hanging out with Chad and his two older brothers, Adam and Daniel, and he and Chad had played varsity baseball together in high school. Still friends, they would often catch a game at The Rusty Tap over beers.

"Hey, how's engagement life?" he asked, prolonging the inevitable release of the blonde spitfire.

Chad grinned. "It's freakin' awesome. You should try it sometime."

"Nah." Jacob shook his head. That wouldn't be happening anytime soon. "I think I'm more suited for the bachelor life. No one to bail out of trouble." His gaze rested on Ashley. "No one to get on your nerves …"

"So, you going to let her go soon?" Chad asked. "I need to drop her off at her condo and then get to the diner. Jen and I have a meeting with the staff to go over the summer menu and update them on the microbrewery."

"How's that going?" Jacob asked. As the manager of Emerald Eats, Chad had recently begun renovations to expand the family diner to include a microbrewery. Jen would soon run the restaurant with him as the brew mistress, a job that apparently she was very good at.

"We'll be opening in five months. Definitely in time for the World Series. Maybe even the playoffs."

Jacob chuckled. "Smart man. What's it going to be called again?"

"Emerald Burgers & Brews. We felt we needed to get 'brew' in there to promote the microbrewery."

"Good call." Jacob could see Ashley attempting to stretch her arms. The cuffs were probably itching her skin at this point.

"How about I talk to Daniel and we'll let the ladies do their Zumba at the resort. Hell, they can do it in the aerobic studio naked if they'd like. No one will see them."

Jacob ignored the tightening of his groin at Chad's suggested compromise and shook his head. Typical Whitman. Always had a quick solution that often involved some location around town. Hell, that was easy—they owned most of the businesses in it.

He continued to watch Ashley, who was now engaged in sweet talk with the intake officer, Mack, behind the counter. Dirty old man. Mack, at sixty, would cave to a pretty face, and Ashley Whitman certainly had one.

Mack—and every guy in Emerald Springs, for that matter—didn't know her like Jacob did. In high school he'd seen right through her as the egotistic, drama queen she was. There, however, was one incident toward the end of their senior year that he chalked up to as a temporary lapse in sanity.

"Come on, Jacob." Chad slapped his back. "Beer's on me if you let her go. We can watch the Sox murder the Yankees. I just brewed some Porch Swing last night."

That got his attention. "The beer with the pear and lime?"

"Grapefruit, ginger, and lime," Chad corrected proudly.

"That's some good shit." Jacob had never intended to arrest Ashley, but Chad's offer sealed the deal. A game and a cold beer or two tonight, catching up with his buddy, sounded good. "Fine. I'll write her up a warning."

"You seriously can't be ticketing me?" Ashley turned and faced him. "I was so right to turn you down in high school. Thank *God* I didn't go to prom with you. You deserved to go alone." Jacob's body tensed. And there it was. The incident he'd buried so deep in the back of his mind, he thought he'd need one of his sister's bulldozers to excavate it, but Ashley had so easily dug the painful memory out with her sharp tongue. He turned and walked past her, motioning to Mack as he headed for the door. "Book her."

The Emerald Springs Legacy Series

Follow the Whitman and Sanders families in their continuing saga as they confront old rivalries and discover new love while protecting their legacy at the Emerald Tea Farm. Look for these upcoming installments in this exciting new continuity series from *Crimson Romance*:

Adam's Ambition by Monica Tillery
Colleen's Choice by Holley Trent
Chad's Chance by Elley Arden
Daniel's Decision by Nicole Flockton
Ashley's Allegiance by Robyn Neeley

To learn more about the Emerald Springs series, visit our website for more details, author interviews, and a special free prequel story.